The Being In The Game

By

Anthony Cole

BaHar
Publishing
1429 Commercial Street
Waterloo, IA 50702

THE EFFECTS OF BEING IN THE GAME
Copyright 2018 by Anthony Cole

First Edition 2020

Published by

BaHar Publishing
1429 Commercial Street
Waterloo, Iowa 50702

Printed in the United States of America

DEDICATIONS

To my loving and supportive mother Ida Roby, who stood by my side while I was doing time. Never once did she complain; what she did instead was share the word of God with me and told me the truth about myself, which was what I needed to help reinvent myself. She helped me shape and mold myself into a Kingdom man.

To my four children who know that they can do anything through Christ Jesus who strengthens them. All I have to say is keep on keeping on. Areyon, who is going to college so that she can help contribute something to people/the world. Kayla, who is also going to college so that she too can make her contribution to the world. Mettia, who's working to provide for her family and working toward one day opening up her own interior decorating business. Tobias, who is working to better his life and looking forward to going to college online.

To my wife Ruth, who has been nothing but a blessing sent from God. To my bonus family: my wife's children Dominiqua, Chelia, Darryl; and my wife's mother, Rosemary.

To my family members which are my aunts, Mary Ann Reed, Sandy Cole, Georgeann Cole and Mattie Cole, who have supported me in many ways. My sisters Stacey Cole, Lisa

Cole, Kristie Roby; and my brothers Terrence Roby, Chris Roby, and Torie Roby.

To my nephew Tyrone Scott who lives in Denver working for the government, and has been a great supporter.

To the rest of my nephews and nieces who are working and running their own businesses: I pray that you all live a life that stands for something.

To my brother from another mother Charlie aka C.B. from Chicago, who has been a true-to-life friend. His mother, Mary G, who has been there for me when I needed someone to talk to. Thank you both for your love and support.

To all of the brothers who are in the belly of the whale/prison doing time and are away from their children and loved ones. Remember that just because they've got your body doesn't mean that you can't still do something meaningful with your lives.

INTRODUCTION

Background on Waterloo, aka 'the city of no love': Waterloo is a city with its own identity that the world had slept on for years, and it has now come out of its grave. A city that was once a place where one could raise a family in a peaceful environment. A city where the residents wanted to see children make something of their lives—and to show them that they had their backs. Many of the concerned citizens opened up non-profit organizations to help the children of their community educationally and recreationally with sports such as basketball, football and wrestling. These organizations led to many young people going off to college on athletic scholarships in these sports. Today, the city that was once known for its citizens coming together to uplift and inspire its young people to go to college has changed. Too many of the young generation have traded away college for becoming drug dealers or gang members.

Waterloo began to change when gang members arrived back in the mid 90's to partake in the lucrative, big city-styled drug trade that the small town had to offer. Eventually, the Chicago lifestyle spilled over into Waterloo, causing the city to become more violent and escalating the drug trade. Waterloo, aka 'the city of no love' was no longer a peaceful and quiet city. A safe place where you could raise a family had turned into a drug and gang war zone. It was no longer safe for children to play anymore, and everyone was feeling the heat of the new generation's action.

From the drug/gang war bodies were piling up in the streets, causing the black community to complain to the city's first-ever elected black mayor, hoping he would do something about it. After hearing non-stop complaints from Waterloo's black citizens, the mayor demands to see something done. The local authorities and the FBI got together and started Operation Take Our City Back. They called citizens on parole or probation for drugs, weapons charges and violent crimes to a grand jury, hoping to get them to give information on the drug trade and gangs. But no matter how hard they tried, the dealers and the gangs were always steps ahead of them.

This story is about five guys from the Westside of Chicago and Chill Will, aka 'Chill' the drug and gang underworld in Waterloo, Iowa aka 'the city of no love'.

As the cousin of the infamous Big El, Chill Will was given the drug connect to keep the family legacy alive while his cousin was in federal prison. It didn't take long for Chill Will—who had been waiting his whole life—to take over the drug empire. He had a competitive mindset and he was so ready to get his feet wet and rub elbows with the rest of the drug elites. Being fresh in the drug game, he knew it wasn't going to be easy for him to climb to the top of the food chain; but was ready to do whatever he had to do to get there. Chill Will knew he was going to need help flooding the city of no love. He started personally picking some local east side childhood friends who had hustled on those streets since they were kids; this led them to forming a crew called the Crip Cartel Operation. The Crip Cartel family stepped into the game thirsting for money and power, which later caused them to bring out the jealousy and hate of many other players in the drug game. The Crip Cartel family had to defend themselves, which led to people getting shot and bodies piling up; the crew that had just wanted money turned into some dangerous killers—and that's when the bodies started to pile up and get hauled off to the morgue.

Food for thought before you get into this book
The question I want to pose to you: Can the game be won?

Can you win a game that is full of jealousy, envy and hate—where everybody's main concern is filling up their cup with money and material things? Can you win a game where people are willing to rob or take someone's life for their money and possessions?

I asked myself the same question that I now ask you all. After looking back on my life experiences and finding out the statistics on how many people are locked up in state and federal prison from being in the game, I have formulated my opinion.

R.I.P to those who lost their lives to gun Violence You are always in your family's thoughts, forever in their hearts, until you meet again in Heaven

Maurice Norris aka butty

Orintheo Campbell Jr.

Shavondes S. Martin aka Buns

Dae Quan "Bubba " Campbell

Otavious Brown

Alonzo Quinn, Rhiannon Olsen & their unborn child Jalen

Tay Deshuan Robinson

Calvin Maurice Rash

Shantorio Vashawn Evans

Randall Randy Scott Dawson

Justin M. Dolen

Denelius House Nesby

John Marvin Parham, Jr.

Rodricus Keith Echols (Jones)

Martavious Tavertos Johnson

Terrence Currington

Taveros "Dino" Dehaun Galloway

Gray Lee Wilson's

Jazz mine Rembert

Derrick Ambrose Jr.

Celio Antonio Posada

Ton'ya Jackson

Greggory Walker

Robert "Little Rob " Robinson

Mikaela Bond Hill

Letter From Heaven

Your loved ones

When tomorrow starts without me,

and I'm not here to see,

If the sun should rise and find your eyes,

filled with tears for me.

I wish so much you wouldn't cry,

the way you did the day I passed away,

while thinking of the many things

we didn't get to say.

I know how much you love me,

as much as I LOVE YOU,

and each time you think of me,

I know you'll miss me too.

When tomorrow starts without me,

don't think we're apart,

for every time you think of me,

I'm right there in your heart.

May God bless all the families that lost a loved one.

May He Bless and Keep you all!

Author Unknown

Prologue

At the age of 16, K'von's uncle, Cuban George was indicted at the federal prison. After K'von graduated from Orr Academy High School along with Moe, Fab and Mo'tik he went off to play basketball on a full ride scholarship at the University of Iowa in Iowa City. After high school, both Moe and Fab enrolled into a community college to study business management because they had planned to open up a clothing store together. After six months in community college they'd decided to drop out to pursue the drug game as a means to getting the money they needed to open up their clothing store.

His other best friend Mo'tik went to play football at Saint Ambrose in Davenport, Iowa; but he had gotten red shirted his freshmen year, even though the coach had sat in his living room and promised him and his parents that he would be starting at quarterback. When the coach didn't keep his promise, Mo'tik became upset with him. The two would argue. Things got so bad, Mo'tik decided to drop out of college and head back to the Chi.

Life had been looking uphill for K'von. He'd been in his second year of college when he had gotten an unexpected, devastating phone call from the mother of his 3-year-old twins Chris and Kristie.

The phone call was about the tragic death of his 3 year-old daughter Kristie, who died from a cocaine overdose. Her mother's boyfriend was selling drugs out of their apartment and had accidentally dropped a piece of crack cocaine on the floor; Kristie had gotten a hold of it and ate it. When K'von got the news, he flew back home to the Chi and never returned to school.

While back at home dealing with the death of his daughter, K'von got an unexpected visit from his childhood friends Moe, Fab, and Mo'tik to pay their respects. At the lowest point in his life, dealing with the death of his 3-year-old daughter, he'd found out that he wasn't alone. Kristie's death had taken a toll on him to the point that he'd become deeply depressed; but his childhood friends had been right there by his side to help him cope with the pain of losing his daughter. Three months had passed since his daughter had been laid to rest, and K'von had started considering what he was going to do to support himself and his three other children, 5-year-old K'von Jr, 2 year-old daughter China, and 3-year-old son Chris, Kristie's twin. He looked for and found a job, but he was let go just a few months later because production was slowing down. Finding himself back at square one, K'von wondered how he was going to take care of his three children and himself. It seemed that as soon as he found hope, he was confronted by war again. With the bills steadily piling up, he needed cash

11

to pay them, and his children needed things. His efforts to find employment seemed not to lead him up, but only further down into the pit. The fact that he struggled to provide food, clothing and shelter for himself and his children had him feeling terribly empty inside. His friends would ask if he needed anything; being so prideful kept him from accepting anything from them. After months of struggling to take care of himself and his children, he'd had enough. One day, he went to his best friends and they put him on. K'von's plan had been to only do it for a little while, because he had seen what the game could do to people. He had come up under his uncle Cuban George, who had been a big-time drug dealer before he and six members of his organization were indicted by the Feds for cocaine and weed trafficking. Cuban George ended up getting popped when a shipment of 100 Kilos was intercepted while being transported in cars and trucks to a car lot he owned in Chicago.

The three men in his organization that were driving the shipment back got busted with the shipment, so they agreed to work with law enforcement. They agreed to drive the shipment back to Chicago to Cuban George, and that's when the Chicago law enforcement and Feds busted him with the 100 Kilos of cocaine. Cuban George ended up with a life sentence due to being charged with the CCE, which carried life in prison because this was his third drug conviction.

K'von and his uncle had become really close after his Pop walked out on his responsibilities as a father to him, Meechie, and their sister. That's when K'von began to look up to Cuban George. They were so close that even prison couldn't separate their bond. Ever since his uncle had been in prison, the two had kept in touch with each other through phone calls, letters and visits.

One day when K'von and his mother went to visit his uncle, his mother told him that K'von had started selling drugs.

"No disrespect Unc, but there is nothing that you can say to me right now that's going to get me to stop doing what I'm doing," K'von told his uncle. "I'm just following in the footsteps of my idol, which is you. "
Cuban George was so hurt by the words he'd heard come from K'von's mouth, a tear rolled down his right eye. He knew firsthand how it felt to lose your freedom and, in his situation, to never to get it again. He had been fighting the government for several years now, and the only chance he had of getting his freedom back was to snitch on his connect in California, Hector.

"Son, here it is: I'm in the fight of my life trying to get out of prison—and here's my *nephew*, throwing rocks at this place trying to get in! As if it is an Ivy League college, and here I am trying to get out! "

When he saw that he wasn't getting through to K'von, he said. "Nephew, if you're going to do it, do it big; because if you get caught they are going to give you as much time as they can. No matter if you sold three Kilos or 100."

Cuban George paused for a minute. "I'll tell you what I'm going to do for you, nephew. I 'm going to hook you up with my connect back in California."

When K'von heard that his eyes lit up and he went to give him a hug. "Thanks, Unc!"

"Hold on now! This is not a game!," he warned. "If you mess up they will kill you, nephew." He gave K'von a number.

"Don't call this number until I call you to let you know that it's a go."

"Thanks again, Unc! I won't let you down," K'von said.

CHAPTER 1

It was a Friday night, and Precious was at home alone watching a movie while her boyfriend K'von was at his nightclub, Vision. After the movie went off Precious started surfing through channels but stopped at a news flash that caught her attention; it was in relation to a police officer who had been dispatched to a home at about 11:00 pm for an armed subject that had been holding people against their will. The news also reported further information that, while holding six hostages against their will, the suspect allegedly assaulted several more people, striking them with his gun while tying them up! The Chicago man, Charles a/k/a Chi Town for about two hours refused to allow anyone to leave the home. After an hour of negotiating with the armed man he finally released two of his hostages, who were quickly questioned by authorities then released to the EMTs for medical treatment of any injuries they may have sustained. After four more hours of negotiation, authorities were able to get him to release the remaining four people. Afterwards, the police rushed in and apprehended Charles a/k/a Chi-Town, who was arrested and charged with six counts of kidnapping. It didn't stop there; the news reported began talking about his past—how Charles a/k/a Chi-Town had been arrested six months prior and charged with attempted murder and robbery after he'd tried to rob a man outside his home. He had slit the victim's neck, causing a severe laceration. Charges from that case were dismissed because the alleged victim had refused to cooperate with law enforcement.

Precious had heard and seen enough; she was tired so she turned the TV off and headed up the stairs to her bedroom. She went to the bathroom to freshen up before going to bed. After that she went into the bedroom, pulled the covers back, kicked off her Fendi slippers and got into her oversized, comfortable bed. Scared from what she had seen on the news, she was unable to sleep right away so she tossed and turned. After about an hour she was finally able to fall asleep.

At around 3:00 am, Precious had only been asleep for about a good hour when she was awakened by a loud noise from downstairs. Panicked by the noise, her heart started racing. She rolled over to see if K'von was in the bed, and she came fully awake when she noticed he wasn't.

She reached into the nightstand drawer for her gun, which she kept for protection just in case something happened while her boyfriend was out and about.

Getting out of bed, she grabbed her robe and started putting it on before going downstairs to investigate the noise. She cocked her gun and just as she was about to leave the bedroom, she looked at the security monitor and saw a disturbing image of a stranger walking around in their spacious, Olympia Fields mansion! The intruder was dressed in black from head to toe, walking around in their kitchen and looking through their drawers. Precious knew right away that it wasn't K'von so she ran over to the bedroom door and locked it, then grabbing her cell phone off of the night stand, she began dialing K'von's number. She was so scared from what she had seen, she started shaking and dropped the phone on the floor. She picked it back up and finished dialing the number, her eyes still glued to the security monitor screen watching the intruder's every move.

K'von's cell just rang and rang. "Please, please answer," she said as his phone kept ringing. There was no answer, just his voice mail saying *"I'm not available right now, but if you leave your name and number, I will get back to you as soon as I can."*

Precious was hurt by her boyfriend K'von for not being there to protect her in dire times as well as being nowhere to be found when she needed him the most. So now she calls her Aunt Helen, who was like a mother to her and had raised Precious as well as her sisters Ashley and A'Lexus, and their brother Marquis ever since they were kids after both their parents had died in a car accident. When she finally reached her Aunt Helen, she immediately said, "Mama, there's someone in the house," in a frantic voice.

"Calm down!" Where's K'von?" Helen asked.

"I don't know."

"Did you call the police?"

"No!"

"I'll call them right now on A'Lexus's cell phone. ", she said.

While her aunt was on the other end calling the police, Precious was watching the intruder go through their belongings. He had now made his way into the living room, where he saw a diamond Rolex left out on one of the end tables. Precious then got very heated because he put it in his bag, because one thing she couldn't stand is a thief. She continued to watch the monitor while listening in on her Aunt Helen still speaking to the 911 dispatcher. But then she noticed the intruder coming up the stairs on the monitor. Now yelling silently into the phone, she asking her Aunt Helen what she should do.

Her aunt couldn't hear her because she was on A'Lexus's cell talking with the dispatcher. As the thief was walking up the stairs Precious had her eyes glued to the screen watching his every move. When the intruder got to the top of the stairs he looked around; he started walking right towards the bedroom where Precious was. When he put his hand on the doorknob and began to turn it, she almost lost it.

"Mom can you hear me?," she said in a low voice, not wanting the intruder to hear her. Her mother didn't answer because she was still on the phone with the dispatcher. Her heart started pounding as if she was about to have a heart attack, and she wondered what was taking her mother so long to speak with the dispatcher.

While waiting for her mom to get back on the phone, Precious began to think of what she could do to scare the intruder off. She was deep in thought; with all the panic, fear of being violated or killed, she had forgotten all about the panic button on the remote that could have stopped the intruder in his early tracks through her home, so she pushed the panic button and it made a very loud noise which startled the intruder. He turned and then raced down the steps and out the back door in a hurry.

By that time, her mother was done talking with the dispatcher. When her mom finished talking to the dispatcher she got back on the phone.

"Help is on its way", she said.

This time it was Precious who didn't respond, because she had her eyes glued to the security monitor, watching and making sure the intruder had left the premises.

"Precious are you still there?',' her mother yelled.

She was so preoccupied with watching the intruder, Precious couldn't hear her mother yelling on the other end of the phone. When she saw that the intruder had left the premises she picked up the phone, and all she could hear was her mother calling her name. *"Precious! Precious!"*

"Mom, I'm okay!"

''What's that noise?''

"It's the alarm."

"Help is on its way, the police should be there in no time, baby girl," her mom said.

"The intruder is gone."

'' How do you know?''

"I saw the intruder racing back down the steps and out the back door. "

"Okay!"

They continued to talk on the phone while waiting for law enforcement to arrive.

About fifteen minutes later there was a knock at the front door. Precious looked at the security monitor and saw two police officers standing at the front door.

"I'll call you back, Mom." She hung up the phone.

She then walked over to the bedroom door, unlocked it and went downstairs. As soon as she opened up the door the officer could see that she was scared and the fat cop asked, "Is everything alright?"

"Yes, sir! Someone just broke into our home."

"We'll take a look around the premises to see if we can find any evidence that the intruder might have left behind," the tall, muscular black cop said.

While the two officers were looking around for evidence, Precious started to feel dizzy so she went into the living room and sat on the couch. She grabbed her phone out of her robe and started dialing K'von's number again. Still no answer;

she was heartbroken all over again. Upset and angry that she couldn't reach her boyfriend, she got up from the couch and started pacing back and forth from the hallway to the living room. After pacing back and forth for about ten minutes she saw what appeared to be headlights coming down the driveway. She knew it was K'von; who else would be pulling up to their crib this late at night?

She walked toward the front door and when she saw that it was him, she took a deep breath, hoping to get herself together; she was so angry, thinking she just might lose her cool. After taking a few deep breaths she began to cool down just a bit. When K'von opened his car door and stepped out, he said, "What are the cops doing at our house?"

From the expression on her face he could tell that she was upset.

"Somebody broke into our home!"

"What?!," he said, in a loud angry voice.

Just as he was about to respond the two officers came walking toward them, he quickly changed up his demeanor.

"Miss, your house is secured," the black cop said to her. "And it looks as if the intruder got in through the back door by picking the lock."

"I wonder why the alarm didn't go off?," K'von said.

The fact that he didn't like cops, K'von turned around and walked into the house while Precious was talking to them.

After the cop was done talking, Precious thanked both of the officers for responding to her call as quickly as they did.

"It's our job to protect and serve," the black cop said.

After thanking them she walked into their home and slammed the front door behind her. K'von was checking the alarm, trying to figure out why it didn't go off when the intruder broke into their home. Precious walked over to the alarm and the first thing that came out of K'von's mouth was, "you forgot to set the alarm."

Precious had just been in a life-threatening situation; and the fact that the first thing K'von said was, *'you forgot to set the alarm'* pissed her off. She was heated.

"Where were you when I needed you?," she asked. "I could have been hurt really bad, raped or killed—who knows what would have happened if that intruder got a hold of me?! And all you can say is that I forgot to set the alarm?!", she said in a loud, angry voice.

Just as he was about to open his mouth to answer her, she began to give him a piece of her mind. He knew he had messed up, and that there was nothing he could do at that point to calm her down, so while she was venting he walked off and she followed right behind him, speaking about the situation that had just occurred.

They ended up in the kitchen, where he went into the fridge and grabbed a bottle of Fiji water. He cracked it open and took a sip.

As he drank, she stood right in front of him with her arms crossed, releasing her anger and frustration about how he had not been there to save her; he just stood there listening. When he took another sip of his water she got so upset that she slapped the bottle of water out of his hand, causing water to splash everywhere. He looked at her and just smiled as she kept talking really fast, because she was so heated at him. She had to stop so that she could catch her breath from all that talking. Just as he was about to apologize to her for not being there to protect her, she interrupted him.

"What if the intruder had gotten a hold of me and raped me, then killed me?," she said, getting his attention and making him think about how bad it could have ended.

He then reached out and grabbed her by the arm, pulling her close toward him; he wrapped his arms around her protectively as he gazed into her eyes, saying, "I'm sorry for not being here when you needed me to protect you, and not answering my cell. I know you probably think I was out cheating on you, but that wasn't the reason for me not answering my cell."

That's what she really was thinking because of the fact that she *had* caught him cheating in the past. The two of them had been together since high school, so Precious already had it in her mind that no matter how much of herself she gave to K'von, he was going to be out there messing around with other females. She was so pissed at K'von she wanted to slap the shit out him, but she did not let the situation get the best of her. Plus, she loved him—and the fact that she had every material thing a woman could ever dream of made her rethink her actions.

"If you weren't out cheating, then why didn't you answer your cell?"

"I've been dealing with something horrible as well," he said.

"Like what?"

"I was dealing with a situation that happened at the club. An underage man died from a cocaine overdose in the restroom, and that's why I wasn't able to answer my phone when you called."

K'von owned an upscale nightclub called Vision in the downtown area of Chicago; after hearing that, her demeanor changed and she began to show sympathy.

"How did this underage person get into the club in the first place?," she asked.

"Your guess is as good as mine," he answered. "The only thing I can think of is that he had a fake ID, because you know my security team wouldn't have let him in if they knew he was underage."

After talking for about an hour or so about what happened at the club, Precious got up out of her chair.

"Both of us have had a long night, so let's go to bed so we can get some rest," she said.

"You're right," he said.

She walked toward the stairs where she stopped to wait for him while he punched in the security code to set the alarm. After setting the alarm K'von walked over to her and gave her a kiss. She then grabbed his hand and the two of them walked up the stairs holding hands.

"I'm going to take a shower before I go to bed," he said.

"I'll be in the bedroom waiting for you to get done," she said with a smile on her face.

While waiting in the bedroom for him to get out the shower she became impatient, so she went into the bathroom to see what was taking him so long.

Just as she was coming through the door he was stepping out of the shower.

"My love, since you're in here won't you make yourself useful by handing me that towel."

She grabbed the towel off the wall rack and began to dry off his back. Once they were done in the bathroom, they quickly climbed into bed, but Precious had sex on her mind and started rubbing on K'von, but he declined, saying,

"Not tonight baby, I'm so tired."

She knew that he was exhausted from dealing with the incident at the club, because he would never pass up an opportunity to make love to her. She just rolled back over onto her side of the bed and went to sleep.

CHAPTER 2

Precious woke up a little before 9:00 the next morning and decided to call a locksmith to see if someone could come out and fix the lock on the back door before the day got started. She was told that the earliest someone could come out to her place was about noon. She climbed back into bed to get a little more rest, because she was still tired from the night before.

About an hour later K'von woke up while Precious was in a deep, relaxed sleep; she was folded up into a Z beside him in the bed. He watched her as she slept, admiring her 5"6 body with long, silky black hair that came down to the middle of her back; her olive skin was flawless. Yes, Precious was a beautiful woman; he began pleasantly caressing her rounded breasts, thighs and backside, setting the mood.

K'von loved to begin his day by having sex with his queen; he believed it set a standard by which to measure the day that unfolded from then on.

After five minutes of him rubbing her all over, Precious rolled towards him and they began caressing each other with their hands and then with their lips, tongues and mouths.

Both of them were enjoying it, when suddenly they were interrupted by the ringing of the doorbell.

"Who could that be, coming to the house this early in the morning?", K'von asked.

"It's probably the locksmith, I called them early this morning to make an appointment to get the back-door lock fixed," Precious answered.

She rose right away, slipping on her pajamas bottoms, a tank top, and her Fendi slippers. She put on her Fendi robe and headed to the front door.

Once at the door, she looked out the peep hole and when she saw that it was someone from the locksmith place, she opened the door.

"Good morning", she said.

"Good morning to you, too. I know that I am a little early, I hope you don't mind."

"I don't mind at all. Follow me," she said.

Precious turned and started walking toward the kitchen and the locksmith followed her. "This is the door that needs to be fixed," she told him.

He looked at the door to assess the damage that had been done to the lock.

"I'll have to replace the entire lock system on this door. "

"That's fine! Do what you need to. Well, I'll let you get to work," she said as she walked off to the kitchen to cook K'von some breakfast.

She opened up the fridge and started grabbing items, and it wasn't long before K'von smelled the aroma of the food. He quickly got up, plunging his feet into his Gucci slippers, and draping his bathrobe around him like a King preparing for the day at hand. K'von went into the bathroom to brush his teeth and wash his face, and when he was done freshening up he proceeded downstairs.

"Good morning my love," he said right before kissing Precious on the lips.

"Good morning to you, too. Have a seat, breakfast is almost ready."

While waiting at the table for her to bring him his plate, K'von couldn't help but think about what had happened at the club the night before. His two main concerns were that the city might try and shut him down, and that the deceased's family might file a lawsuit against him. The fact that both things could happen began to tug on his conscience. K'von was so deep in thought about it, he couldn't even hear his girl calling him. All of sudden he felt a tap on his right shoulder, and looked up.

"Is everything alright?"

"Yes! Why do you ask that?"

"Because I called your name several times, and you didn't answer."

"Sorry, baby! I was just deep in thought, thinking about something."

"I hope it was about the nightclub incident."

"Yes!"

"First and foremost, what happened to the young man was devastating," Precious said. "The fact that it wasn't your fault, I believe that you shouldn't be held accountable for his actions."

"You're right, but the victim's family might try to blame his death on me, seeing that I am the owner of the club," K'von replied.

"If they do, you have lawyers to take care of your legal matters; and also in your favor, K'von, this has been the only incident that has ever happened in the club within the five years since you've been open. I don't see them shutting the club down—so quit stressing about it. Now, just relax and let your high-paid lawyers take care of it," she said.

"You are so right," he said as she was handing him his plate. "This looks good."

Trying to mentally distance himself from the situation—at least for awhile—he placed a forkful of eggs into his mouth, then sipped his coffee. While she was fixing her plate so she could join him, he said, "thank you, my love, for being so supportive."

"You're welcome! As your woman, it's my duty to love and support you no matter what."

She turned and walked over to the table, put down her plate, then gave him a kiss. Just as she was about to pull out her chair from underneath the table, he stopped her.

"Let me get that for you," he said. He pulled the chair out for her and she sat down.

"You're such a gentleman!," she said with a big smile on her face.

While they were sitting at the table enjoying breakfast together, K'von took a bite of his turkey bacon and then reached for his toast. Before he took another bite of his toast, he put it back on his plate and stood up.

"What's wrong?, " Precious asked.

"Nothing! I'll be right back," he said as he walked away.

He went to check on the locksmith guy. When he walked into the room, K'von paid close attention to how hard the man was working at getting the locks fixed; the man didn't even notice K'von standing behind him.

K'von stood there for a couple of seconds watching him work.

"Make sure you give us the best lock money can buy."

"Yes sir," the locksmith said, then turned around and went back to working on the door.

K'von stood there for few seconds watching the man put the new lock on the door; he then walked back into the kitchen and sat back down at the table to finish breakfast with his girl.

"Where did you go?"

"I went to see if the locksmith needed anything," K'von answered.

Precious looked at him and smiled, because she knew that was a lie; she knew he didn't trust anybody who wasn't family or a part of his circle. Everyone else was suspect.

"Let the man do his job. The more you bother him, the longer it's going to take him to fix the lock," she said.

The two went back to eating their breakfast. Just as they were about finished eating, the locksmith walked into the kitchen and knocked on the wall to get their attention. The both of them turned around.

"I'm finished with the lock," he announced.

"That was quick! I thought it would have taken you at least a few hours," K'von said.

"Probably for those who don't know what they are doing," the locksmith said.

They both got up from the table to go look over his work. With Precious following right behind him, K'von walked straight over to the door and started inspecting the locksmith's work. The way he was looking over it, you would have thought he was a USDA inspector.

"It looks great! I'm satisfied with it," he said. "What do you think, Precious?"

"I think he did a nice job. I really do like this new lock system."

"What do I owe you for this fine job you've done here today?"

The man pulled out his calculator and he began to punch in some numbers.

'Your total is $750.00 dollars."

"I'll be right back!"

K'von walked off, heading upstairs to the bedroom for cash to pay the man.

While he was upstairs getting the money, the locksmith started packing up his belongings. When K'von returned, he handed him $950 dollars in cash and he began to count it.

"Sir, the bill is $750 dollars; you gave me $200 dollars too much."

'I know, it's a tip. You did such a wonderful job that I wanted to give you a blessing. You know, it is true what they say about God; He knows what we need even before we ask," K'von said to the man.

"Thank you sir," the locksmith replied.

K'von then escorted him to the door and just as he was about to leave, the man thanked K'von one last time. He extended his hand to K'von and the two shook hands. After K'von closed the door he walked back into the kitchen. Precious was cleaning off the table, and he walked right up to her and gave her a kiss on the cheek.

'What was that for?"

"For the amazing breakfast you cooked, and for being such an amazing soul mate."

'Aww, that's so sweet of you to say about me!"

"Look here babe, I've got a meeting with my employees at the club to talk about the incident that happened last night. We need to see how we can prevent something like this from happening in the near future. But once the meeting is over, I promise I'm all yours."

"Okay, just make sure you call me before you leave the meeting so I can be ready when you get back. "

"I surely will," he said, and then he went upstairs to get dressed.

CHAPTER 3

After the meeting ended, K'von called Precious to let her know that he was on his way. On the drive back to the house, he began to think about how blessed he was to have someone like Precious in his life; she was a good woman, and he knew that good women were hard to come by these days. So, to let her know that he loved and appreciated her, he decided to stop by the flower shop.

He pulled into the parking lot of the florist, went inside, and he purchased a dozen long-stemmed red roses for his sweetheart.

While he was at the counter paying for the roses, the cashier asked him, "what's the special occasion?"

He looked at her with a big smile on his face and said, "no special occasion...I just want to express my appreciation and love for my wonderful girlfriend."

"That's so nice of you," the cashier said.

After paying for the roses, he got back into his car and drove out of the parking lot, on his way to pick up Precious. When he was about three blocks from home his cell phone rang. He grabbed it and when he saw that it was a private number, he knew right away that it was Too Cool, who was friends with K'von's uncle Cuban George. Too Cool, who was a big-time drug dealer in his former life, had gotten locked up a year

34

ago for shooting some guy who'd tried to rob him at gunpoint for his drugs.

He accepted his call. "What's going with you, Slick?"

"Nothing much, just doing time. Man, I can't wait until this sh*t is over," Too Cool said.

"How much longer you got?," K'von asked him.

" Less than a year and half, Slick."

"That time will fly by faster than you know it."

"How's life treating you on the outside?," Too Cool asked him.

" Life is treating me pretty well, I must say."

"I been hearing about you."

K'von cut him short and said, "man, you and I both know you can't believe nothing that you hear."

" Look here Slick, I called you to see if you could do me a solid."

" What is it?"

"I need you to send me Pimpin' Ken's new book called 'Art of the Human Chess'."

"Say no more, it's done. I will send some money for canteen as well."

"Thank you, I sho' appreciate that."

While he was talking, a recording came on and it said, *'you have one more minute until this call is terminated'.*

The two then said their goodbyes right before the call ended.

By that time, K'von was pulling into his long driveway. He called Precious to let her know that he was outside. While he was waiting for her to come out, he looked through his CD case for his Maxwell CD.

When he heard the front door open, he looked; when he saw her dressed in her Louboutin shoes, Balmain skirt with a matching top, and her oversized Gucci bag strapped around her arm, he just lit up. He loved it when she dressed up. She looked like a supermodel every time! Being the gentlemen that he is, he got out of the car and opened the door for her.

"You look so beautiful, my queen!"

"Thank you!"

When she got into the car he closed the door behind her, walking back around to the driver's side. She reached over the seat and opened the door for him, and he got in.

"I have a surprise for you."

He then reached into the back seat to grab the roses. "These flowers are for you, my beautiful flower," he said as he handed them to her.

"Aww, you're so sweet," she said before thanking him with a kiss on the lips.

As K'von pulled out of the driveway, he asked, "now, where are we off to?"

"To the nail shop to get manicures and pedicures," she said, which both of them liked to do as a couple from time to time.

"I know you probably thought that whatever my plans were, they were all about me, didn't you?"

"No, it never crossed my mind," he said. "I know what type of woman I have gotten into the bed with. A woman who has a heart of gold. You know that's one of the things that I admired about you when we first started dating. At first, I couldn't understand why you were so eager to help people, especially those that you didn't know."

"Well, K'von, I was raised in the church and we were taught to be Christ-like. You were raised in the streets more so than in the church. You were taught not to trust anybody, because everyone is a potential suspect or out to get you—that's why you couldn't understand why I would go out of my way to help people."

"You're right! But it wasn't like that in the beginning; I did trust others up until my father abandoned me, my brother Meechie and our sister Tasha. Growing up, I was taught that your parents were basically like God in the flesh. They were the ones who were supposed set the example for you, protect you and teach you the values of life. As for my father, he dropped the ball and when he abandoned our family, *that's* when I became bitter and angry.

With the one who was supposed to teach me how to be man left out of the picture, I went to the streets in search of a father figure so I could learn how to be a man. And one of the things that I picked up along the way was not to trust anybody, because trust could get you killed. I also learned that trust was something that needed to be earned. Not to get off of subject, but I must admit that living by the code of 'don't trust nobody' has kept me in the game longer than many."

"You're right; it has made you more cautious about life, which has made you a great thinker. I believe it has allowed you to take the game to another level."

While she was speaking a tear rolled down his left cheek, and he wiped it off.

"Did I just see a tear?"

"Nah, it just my allergies acting up."

"Allergies, my butt."

"We're not that far from Fancy nail salon," he said, taking the focus off himself.

"You think you're slick, I know what you're doing."

K'von pulled into the parking lot of the nail salon, which was packed; he drove around through the lot looking for a parking spot. Once he found a space, he put the car in park, shut off the engine and exited the vehicle. As they were walking off he pushed the button to the car alarm, making sure it was secured.

When they got to the door of the nail salon K'von opened the door for Precious. As soon as the owner of the salon spotted them walking through the doors, she walked up to them with a smile on her face, greeting them as royalty, saying, "Precious, you and K'von can come right this way," and escorted them to their seats.

After they sat down the owner of the nail salon began to work on Precious' manicure while another employee started working on K'von. While Precious was getting her nails worked on she looked over at her man.

"Isn't this so nice and relaxing?"

"Yes, it is! I needed this, I must say."

About half an hour into getting pampered, K'von was done and was on his way to get his pedicure. Precious wasn't even close to being finished with her manicure, because she was getting all kinds of fancy designs on her nails.

K'von got out of the chair and headed over to the pedicure station. When he walked past Precious, he said, "I'm done already."

He sat down in the chair and put his feet into the water. The lady began to work on his toes right away. It didn't take her longer than 30 minutes to give him a pedicure.

After he finished, he looked over at Precious to see how far along she was; she still wasn't close to being done, so he walked over to her and said, "I'm about to step outside to get some fresh air."

"Okay!," she said.

He looked at his watch to see what time it was. When he got outside, he reached into his pocket, pulled out his cell phone and started to dial his mother's number.

"Hey son, what's going on?"

"Nothing much Mom, just spending some quality time with Precious."

"That's a good thing, son—but the way you said it made it sound like it wasn't. Is everything alright, son?"

"Yea, everything is fine! I've just got a lot on my plate that I'm dealing with right now, that's all."

"Are you talking about that incident that happened at your nightclub the other night?"

"Yes! " How did you know about that?"

"Precious called me up and told me all about it because she was concerned about you. She saw how it was stressing you out, so don't get mad at her for mentioning it to me. The girl loves you son, and she was only looking out for your best interest. Stop worrying about it, and just enjoy your quality time with Precious."

"Thanks for the words of encouragement, Mom.'"

"You're welcome, son! You know one of my jobs as a mother is to support you when you're dealing with something, no matter how old you are."

"You're the best, Mom! Not to change subjects, though; but my reason for calling you was to ask you for a favor. "

"Anything for you, son. What is it?"

"I need you to let my chef Tony into the house so that he can cook dinner for Precious and I. After we are done spending the day together, I want to surprise her with a special meal."

"That's so nice of you, son; I can do that. Does she know you're doing this for her?"

"No! It's going to be a nice surprise, too."

"What do you have planned for him to prepare?"

"Steak, Shrimp, Lobster, all of her favorites."

"Alright, son," she said, and hung up the phone.

K'von didn't mind leaving Tony unattended in his house until he and Precious arrived, because he had a state-of-the-art security system that recorded his every move. Plus, Tony had been his chef for years and had never shown any sign of betrayal.

When K'von got off the phone with his mother, he went back into the salon.

Precious was just finishing up. "What took you so long?," she asked.

"I was talking to my mom. You know how she is when she gets to talking."

"She *is* long-winded," Precious said.

"Wait until I talk to her, I'm going to tell her what you said, too."

"Don't do that K'von, you know how she is! She will take it very personal."

He just laughed, because he knew she was so right.

As they were walking out of the salon door, K'von asked, "where are we off to now?"

"To the mall, I need to pick up few items."

When they got to the car he opened the door for her so that she didn't break a nail. He shut the door, walked over to driver's side and got in. He put the key into the ignition of his S 600 Benz and started it up.

Once he hit the freeway he started to speed up, going in and out of lanes. He looked over at Precious, and she smiled.

"When are you going to make me your wife?," she asked him.

He was startled by her question because he hadn't expected her to ask him that. There was a pause and then a long sigh before he finally spoke.

"Where did that come from?," he asked.

"Just answer the question," she replied.

He took a minute to take it all in; and what came out of his mouth was shocking to Precious.

"Let's set a date," he said.

"Are you serious?"

"Yes! I'm serious."

This is what Precious had been waiting for all her life: for him to say yes, he will marry her. She was so excited that she reached over and gave him a kiss, then put her arms around his neck for a hug, which caused the car to drift into the left lane, almost causing an accident.

K'von quickly got control of the wheel and switched back over into the right lane.

"Good thing there was no car in the other lane, or we would have been dead or in the hospital," he said.

"Sorry, Bae, I was caught off guard by your response and I got excited...are you serious?," she asked him for the second time.

"Yes, my queen; I think it's long overdue that I make you my wife. You are so worthy of being my wife. Why should I make you wait any longer for your dream to become true? You have always wanted to be Mrs. Coleman."

"I love you, K'von," she said in a low, sexy voice.

"I love you, too!" She leaned over and gave him another kiss on the cheek; she was so excited that she was about to get married.

"I can't wait to tell my Aunt Helen the great news!"

Precious was 5 years old when her parents had died in a car accident 22 years ago; Aunt Helen had become mother to her and her other three siblings after their parents died.

Precious dialed Aunt Helen's number and blurted out the news as soon as she answered.

"Me and K'von is getting married, Mom!," she said with excitement.

"That's wonderful news!," she said. *"Make sure to include me in planning your wedding."*

"You know I will. How could I leave out the angel who rescued me and my siblings decades ago?"

"I'm not an angel, but I am honored that you call me one. Family is everything, and your mother was not only my big sister she was my best friend too. Taking you guys in was an honor."

"Thank you, Aunt, for being a wonderful friend to me, a great aunt, and amazing mother as well."

While she was on the phone talking to her aunt, K'von was deep in thought about the fact that he'd just said yes to getting married.

K'von wanted to marry Precious, just not right now. He'd only said yes because he felt that if he didn't, he was going to lose the love of his life. He had a plan; and it was to drag the wedding date out as long as he could.

Finally, they made it to the mall and he found a parking space right away. They got out of the car and started walking toward the main entrance holding hands.

As they were walking into the mall, Precious said, "How about we meet back up here in an hour."

Precious had a few things she wanted to pick up, and she didn't want him to see the surprise that she had planned for him later.

"Okay that's fine, because I know how you get when you're around clothes and shoes."

They went their separate ways to do some shopping.

As Precious was walking through the mall she was smiling from ear to ear; she was so ecstatic about K'von saying yes to them getting married—and what she had planned for her man later on that night.

Her first stop was at Victoria's Secret to pick out a few sexy items. She looked around for the perfect outfit that would just make K'von's eyes roll into the back of his head. After looking around for about half an hour or so, she found what she believed to be the perfect outfit. It was a sexy, royal blue bra and panties set. Since royal blue was his favor color, she just knew he was going to love it. Plus, it showed off her best assets—her breasts, butt, and flat stomach. On her way to the register she came across a red one-piece; being that red was *her* favorite color, she decided to purchase it.

When she got to the cash register she had about five customers in front of her. Knowing she was pressed for time, she looked at her watch.

She noticed that she had been in Victoria's Secret for about 45 minutes. The line was now down to three customers, and another cashier who'd just come back from break opened up another register; she hopped right in her line.

"Did anybody help you with your purchases?," the cashier asked as she rang her items up.

"No."

"You have lovely taste, by the way," the cashier said. "Your total is $159.97," she said after she rung up her last item.

Precious reached into her Gucci purse and pulled out a credit card from her Gucci wallet, and put her credit card into the machine.

Once the transaction was done, the cashier handed Precious her bags. As she was handing her the bags she said, "thanks for shopping at Victoria's Secret."

"Thank you for thanking me," she said before walking away.

After she left the store, she headed over to an expensive store called R& S Ties to purchase a tie for her man. After about twenty minutes of looking, she found what she believed was the perfect tie. She picked it up and headed right to the register to pay for the tie.

She was on her way to meet up with her man when she came across a new department store called Designers. It was like Saks in New York, and with her weakness for clothes, shoes and handbags, she decided to check it out to see what they had.

"Hi, my name is Jen, and welcome to Designers," a sales associate said as soon as she stepped foot in the department store. "If I can be of any assistance, please let me know."

"Oh, thank you!," she said. "How long have you guys been open?," she asked the lady.

" Just a little while—a month today, to be exact."

As Precious looked around the store, she started to grab all kinds of items that she liked. She grabbed 2 Nicole Miller pantsuits, 3 pairs of designer jeans, 2 Fendi jogging suits, and shoes to match the outfits; 2 pairs of Valentino shoes, 2 pairs of Jimmy Choo designer shoes and 2 each of Christian Louboutin and Louis Vuitton bags.

While she was in Designer on a shopping spree, K'von was blowing her cell phone up, but she just ignored it and keep right on shopping. She had already told him that he owed her big time, and shopping was part of it.

Since Precious didn't answer her phone, K'von thought it would be a good time to call his mother to see how thing were coming along with Chef Tony cooking dinner for him and Precious.

"Hey son, where are you guys at?"

"We're still at the mall, Mom. How's everything going?"

"Everything is fine! Tony is doing a wonderful job, and the food looks so amazing," she said. *"How long do you think it will be before you two get here?"*

"I don't know, so let me call you back after I talk to Precious."

After he hung up the phone he called Precious, who was standing in line waiting to pay for her items.

"Where are you at?" he said.

"I'm on my way to the food court to meet you right now."

"You're okay! I was calling to see what else you had planned for us to do today, because I just got off the phone with my mother; she said she needed to speak with me right away and that it was urgent."

"Is everything alright?," she asked.

" I don't really know; she didn't really say much except that it was urgent."

" Well, the only other thing that I had wanted to do after we leave the mall was go to my favorite restaurant, but it can wait. Your mother takes precedence over my favorite restaurant. We can do that another time."

"Thank you for being so understanding bae," he said.

Once he hung up the phone, he called his mother back.

While K'von was dialing his mother's number, Precious had pulled out her credit card waiting for her total. When the cashier told her the total, she just handed over the credit card as if it was nothing.

While she was spending K'von's money, he was on the phone talking with his mother.

"Mom, ask Tony how much more time he needs to finish cooking?"

She walked into the kitchen and said, "Tony, K'von wants to know how much time you need to prepare the feast."

"About an hour or so, son."

"That's perfect, Mom, because it will take us a least an hour to get back to our house. Thanks for everything, Mom. You're the best."

When K'von got off the phone, he then called Precious.

"Where are you?," he asked.

"I'm walking past Mr. Kay's," she answered, which was a lie because she was actually in the store, looking for a suit for him.

About 5 minutes later she came walking around the corner, and he was sitting down drinking some lemonade. When he saw all those shopping bags in her hands, he just smiled.

"Is there anything in those shopping bags for me?"

"You have to wait until we get home and see," she said.

He opened the door for her, and as the two of them walked out she said, "I love you."

"I love you too, my love."

Being the gentleman that he was, when they got to the car he pushed the trunk button on his car alarm and she put her bags in the trunk. He then opened the car door for her and she got inside and they drove off.

Pulling out of the parking lot, K'von looked over at his girl and asked her, "What all did you buy?"

"It's a surprise!," she said. "Just know that when you see it, it's going to make your heart skip a beat. It might even make your eyes roll into the back of your head as well."

"Now, that sounds like a surprise for real."
While driving down the freeway, he was doing 20 miles over the speed limit.

"You need to slow down," she said.
She always complained about his driving, so he just ignored her and kept right on speeding. About 5 miles up the road, a cop hit the siren on his squad car and pulled K'von over on the side of the highway.

"I told you to slow down," she said.
The cop got out of his squad car and walked over to the passenger's side window to keep from being hit by a passing car. He knocked on the window and Precious rolled it down. He looked at K'von and said, "Can I see your license, and proof of insurance, Sir?"
K'von reached into his pocket and pulled out his license, then reached into the glove box and grabbed his proof of insurance. He handed both of them to the cop.

"Could you explain to me why you were doing 90 in a 70?," the cop asked.

"Officer, can I step out of the car to talk to you in private, please?"

"Yes, you can!'

He got out of the car and began to explain to the officer why he was speeding.

"Sir, my fiancée's mother is really sick, and I was trying to get her to hospital so she could be by her mother's bedside."

"Son, I like the fact that you are concerned about her mother, but that still doesn't give you the right to drive over the speed limit."

"You're right, it doesn't, I apologize!"

"I don't want to hold you up any longer than I already have. So, if everything checks out, I will let you be on your way."

"Thank you, sir! ''

The cop walked back to his squad car to run his name in the system. About 3 to 5 minutes went past and he walked back to his car.

"Everything checks out so you are free to go, but make sure you drive the speed limit—being considerate of others driving on the highway as well."

K'von was so happy that he had gotten off with just a warning. He pulled back onto the road with caution; he was on his way to the book store to buy "The Art of the Human Chess" by Pimpin Ken for Too Cool, and to Western Union to send off the money he'd promised him. Both places were next door to each other in the plaza area, so he was able to kill two birds with one stone. He had Precious to go purchase the book while he went inside Western Union. Since there was a line with about four people, he called his mother to see if Tony was done cooking.

"He's just about done, son," she told him.

"That's perfect! Look here Mom, I want you to set the table for us and pull out a bottle of white wine from my collection for us."

"Will do, son."

"Mom, there's been a change of plans. I was going to have Chef Tony serve us, but I decided to do it myself. So, let Tony know and make sure you guys lock up the house when you leave," K'von said. "And tell Tony I said thanks also. Thank you for everything too, Mom."

"You're welcome, son."

After the Western Union transaction went through, they got back into his car and headed home.

It took them about twenty minutes to get to the house. When he pulled into the driveway he could see that his mother and Tony had already left. The two of them got out of the car he grabbed her bags. She unlocked the front door, and they could smell the aroma of the food in the air as soon as she opened the door.

"Something smells good." she said.

"It sure does, I wonder what it is?," he replied.

Precious walked towards the kitchen and when she walked past the dining room she saw the spread that Chef Tony had prepared for them. The table was set for two.

" You did all this for me?," she asked, surprised.

"Yes, I did!"

"You're such an amazing man. Thank you, so much! I love you more than words can express."

She was so full of joy over what her man had gone out his way to do for her, she began kissing him passionately.

"Save that for later, because I got something that I been dying for you to put your lips on."

"You are so nasty," she said.

He then slapped her on her butt. "Now go put your bags up."

She grabbed all of her bags and up the steps she went. After putting her bags away, she went into the bathroom to freshen up. After she was done she headed back downstairs to enjoy the feast with her man. Being the gentleman that he is, K'von pulled out her chair for her and she sat down. He fixed her plate before making his own, then sat at one end of the table while she sat at the other. Even though her man was a drug dealer, she still did not let that keep her from honoring God.

"Let's pray before we eat," she said; she was taught that one must honor God in all things. Precious prayed over the food in the name of Jesus.

After she was done praying K'von opened the wine and poured her a glass, then one for himself before sitting back down. The two enjoyed their feast and sipped on some white wine.

As they ate and enjoyed each other's company, Precious said, "K'von you're the best man in the whole world. You have treated me like a queen from day one. I've never met a man as wonderful as you, my King."

K'von was so touched by what she'd had to say about him, he had to say something.

"My love, you're the best thing that has ever happened to me. You are my sun when I wake up in the morning and my moon at night that gives me comfort and helps me be able to sleep in peace at night. You are my rock as well," he told her.

"You really mean that, K'von?"

"Yes, I do! I couldn't begin to imagine life without you. You are my soul mate, and I knew it back when we first started dating in the ninth grade."

K'von was not the type who would openly express his feelings; Precious was shocked that he was opening up to her like he was. Pushing her chair back from the table, she walked over to him with tears in her eyes, giving him a big, wet kiss on the lips.

"K'von I can't imagine life without you, either."

She sat back down, and they ate until they were full and sipped on wine until they were tipsy.

He excused himself from the table and went upstairs to the bathroom to fill the Jacuzzi. After it was full, he went back downstairs to join her.

"Who's going to do the dishes?," she asked him.

"I will," he answered, and he started cleaning off the table and putting the dishes into the dishwasher. Being that she was a team player—and K'von had done more than enough to make up for not being there when the intruder broke into their home--Precious decided to help with the dishes.

"I got this, babe," he insisted. "Why don't you go upstairs and relax in the Jacuzzi? I'll join you in just a few minutes."

"Alright," she said in a sexy sweet voice, then turned around and headed upstairs.

When she walked into the bathroom and saw candles lit and rose petals floating around in the water, she couldn't believe it; she hadn't seen this romantic side of him in years. She undressed and got into the Jacuzzi.

K'von had just finishing putting the dishes into the dishwasher and was ready to go upstairs and join his significant other. He went to the fridge and grabbed the whipped cream and some strawberries, and put them on a silver tray as he walked away. In a hurry to be with Precious in the Jacuzzi, he almost forgot to get the wine. He reached for it on the kitchen counter top, and with wine in hand, he headed right back up the stairs and into the Jacuzzi with Precious.

When he walked into the bathroom with the tray of strawberries her eyes lit up. He placed the tray on the edge of the Jacuzzi.

"Look at you, Mr. Romantic. I hope that this will be an ongoing thing," she said.

"It depends on you," he responded.

She then raised her left leg out of the water into the air. As water dripped down, she gave him a sexy look as she licked her lips. "Come join me!"

After seeing her naked body in the Jacuzzi, he wasted no time getting undressed. The whole time he was undressing she was licking on her right breast, sparking an intimate wild fire inside of him.

After rubbing and touching all over each other and feeding one another strawberries in the Jacuzzi, they finished off the rest of the bottle of wine from dinner. Precious really wasn't a drinker, and K'von could tell that the wine was starting to kick in and rev up her sex drive. She stroked his manhood until he got aroused, which led them to intertwine their bodies as one. At this point K'von had had enough, and he was so ready to make love to the love of his life. He lifted her out of the water and said, "let's take this to the bedroom."

He got out of the Jacuzzi, then grabbed her arm and helped her out. They then took turns drying each other off.

When she walked into the bedroom she went straight to the foot of the bed, stopped and turned her back to their

56

oversized bed, and fell gracefully on her back. Once she hit the bed she looked at him and spread her arms and legs wide, as if she were an angel. He walked towards her and when he got to the bed and reached out to grab her, she placed her leg right in the center of his chest and stopped him.

"Not until I show you my surprise. I'll be right back," she said, and then got up from the bed and walked into their big walk-in closet, closing the door behind her. He could hear her going through the shopping bags.

When she returned, she had on just her lace La Perla, royal-blue matching bra and thong, and the tie she'd bought for him around her neck. The royal blue lace bra and thong perfectly complemented her complexion. His eyes lit up as if he had just hit the lottery.

" You like what you see, my king?," she asked him in her sexy tone.

He just sat speechless as she stood there looking like a Victoria's Secret model.

"What's the matter, cat got your tongue?"

"Nah...you just look so gorgeous in that royal blue," he said.

She walked over to the bed, stopped right in front of it, and crawled in with him. They began to kiss passionately. K'von extended his tongue into her mouth and she began sucking on it gently.

After a few more passionate kisses on the lips, K'von started to work his way down to her chest, then her stomach. He didn't stop there; he continued working his way down her body. He grabbed the can of whipped cream and right before he sprayed it, he said "I like my desert with whipped cream on top. "

He shook the can, then sprayed whipped cream on her body.

While making love to his girl K'von's cell phone rang, and he just let it ring. But when whoever it was called back a second time, he told Precious right in the middle of making love to her, "I have to answer this call."

"Don't stop!"

As much as he wanted to sexually please her, he took the call because it might have been something important. He rolled off her and grabbed his phone.

"*Where are you?,*" Meechie said.

"At home," K'von answered. "Why?"

"*Big bro, we have a problem...one of my soldiers named Slug was killed today.*"

"What happened?"

"*Him and his chick was coming out of her apartment building on their way to the movies, and two guys approached him with guns saying this is a robbery—give it up, don't make it a homicide,*" Meechie explained. "*After taking his money and jewelry, they still killed him.*"

"Bro, I know how you are about spilling blood in the streets, so that's why I'm calling you: to let you know that we are going to handle this...we got to send a message to let people know that if you mess with one of ours, there's going to be some repercussions."

"Do what you got to do, family. "

When K'von hung up from talking to his brother Meechie, he walked back into the bedroom to join Precious who was lying across the bed, butt naked. He just knew that she had a whole lot to say to him about taking a phone call while they were in the middle of making love. Surprisingly, she didn't; but he could tell by the look on her face that she had lost her sex drive.   They ended up watching a movie because K'von had to be at the club later on.

After Meechie hung up from K'von he started making phone calls to see if anybody knew who the two guys were who had killed his boy Slug. Being well- connected in those streets, it didn't take him long to find out the names of the two guys who killed Slug. Once he put the word out that there was a reward for any information leading to their whereabouts, the streets started spilling their guts. The killers were twin brothers named Tyrone and Tyron. Once Meechie got their names and address he started to plan deaths right away. The two were still staying with their mother, but that meant nothing to Meechie; in his mind, if she was there when they got handed down their punishment for killing one of his, she could get it too. Meechie wasn't in the business of killing someone else's mother because he too had a mother, but if he had no choice he would.

Meechie sent four of his most notorious young soldiers to scope out the twins' mother's crib. Before they left he had told them to make sure not to leave any witnesses—meaning, kill the twins' mother too, if she was there. When the four of them made it to the address, they waited outside the crib for the twins to come home. After waiting outside for about two hours the twins finally showed up. Meechie's soldiers crept up on them while one of the twins was putting his key into the lock at the side door. One of the soldiers, John-John, slapped one of the twins upside the head with his pistol and he fell to his knees. Mike and the other two soldiers pointed their guns at the other twin's head. Once the door was open they stepped inside and went into the basement, which was a few feet from the door.

"Go check the rest of the crib," Mike said to Gunner and D' Mack. While they were checking out the crib to make sure that nobody else was in the house, Mike punched Tyron in his stomach, causing him to fall to his knees; vomit came spewing out of his mouth.
He hit him again in the jaw, causing him to spit blood. When John-John looked around and saw the other twin brother, Tyrone looking at him sideways.

'What the fuck you looking at?"

Mike was standing behind Tyrone and when he heard that, he kicked Tyrone in the back of his knees and he hit the floor, falling flat on his face. Mike then grabbed him by the back of his shirt and pulled him back up on his knees. He got in Tyrone's face.

"Listen nigga, this is karma catching up with you for killing Slug," Mike said.

"I didn't kill Slug," Tyrone answered.

By that time, Gunner and D' Mack had finished searching the house. When Tyrone said that, the two of them surrounded him with their guns pointed in his face. They knew he was lying.

"You're a lying-ass nigga," Gunner said right before he hit him in the nose with the butt of his gun, causing blood to come gushing from his nose.

"Fuck this, let's do what we came here to do," D 'Mack said. He walked over to Tyron, put the barrel of his Glock to his head, and pulled the trigger. Blood came spewing from his head. After watching his brother get shot Tyrone was so scared he pissed on himself. He then began to plead for his life, blaming it all on his brother.

"It was my brother who killed your boy Slug, please don't kill me!"

"It was your brother, huh," Mike said.

"Yes!"

"Well since you guys are twins I can't tell who is who, so I guess I have to kill you too, because I can't tell the difference."

Just as John-John was about to off him, Gunner stopped him.

"Let me kill him, I haven't killed nobody in a month."

"He's all yours then," John-John said, and stepped aside to let Gunner handle his business. Gunner walked up on him and he jumped.

"What you jumping for? You weren't scared when you killed our boy Slug." Then he kicked him in the nuts. He hit the floor face first, and that's when Gunner stood over him and shot him twice in the head. Blood was leaking from everywhere—his mouth, the back of his head. As they were about to leave Mike saw some lighter fluid on a shelf on the wall and picked it up.

"Let's burn their bodies so that their mother won't be able to recognize them."

He opened the lid and began to squirt the fluid all over their bodies. Once he was finished he lit a rag that was on the floor and threw it on them; the four of them watched the bodies burn for a few seconds then left. Back at K'von's crib the movie over and it was time for him to get dressed so that he could go to his club. He got up and started to get dressed. He grabbed his shirt and put it on, then started putting on his custom, tailor-made Armani suit. Next came his wingtip

Ferragamo loafers and his H Hermes belt. To put the icing on the outfit, he grabbed the gold Rolex from his expensive watch collection and put it on his wrist.

"How do I look?," he asked Precious.

"Like a true boss."

He wanted to see for himself so he walked over to the floor-length mirror and looked into it. He turned back around and looked at Precious..

"I'm sharp as shit," he said.

He gave her a goodbye kiss, walked out of the bedroom and out the front door, on his way to his nightclub.

CHAPTER 4

K'von was pulling into his club's parking lot. He noticed that Meechie's black Range Rover with red leather interior; Moe's black-on-black S 550 Benz; Fab's silver Yukon Denali with custom royal blue interior; and Mo'tik black Cadillac Escalade truck with custom red seats were parked all in a row. He parked his car in his reserved space and headed toward the door. When he walked through the door of the club, he could see that his employees were busy getting ready for tonight. Even though that young man had had a cocaine overdose in the club the other night, K'von wasn't going to let that get in the way of him making his money.

"Hello everyone," he said to his employees when he walked into the club.

Big T approached him. "Meechie, Fab, Moe and Mo'tik are in your office waiting for you," he said.

He knew they were there, after seeing their vehicles when he drove into the parking lot. Plus, the five of them always met at the club to discuss business anyway, so that was nothing new.

"Thanks for letting me know. Make sure everything gets done, Big T," he said as he was walking to his office to meet with his GMO brothers.

"I will boss, you know you can count on me."

K'von had a loyal and hardworking team of men whom he could trust and count on, which was important in his line of work. What made them unique was that they all brought something different to the GMO empire and all their characters complemented each other. For instance, take Meechie; he was the wild and smooth type. He was the youngest of the GMO Gettin Money Operation, but he was smart too. He had his own squad of young juveniles who knew how to check that bag, and they were hitters who weren't scared to pull that trigger. He had them pushing weed like crazy in their high schools and on those west side corners. He had other customers that bought weight as well. As for Mo'tik, he was more of the player type. Fab was laid back, and he was also business educated. Moe was the observant one; you couldn't get anything past him no matter how hard you tired. As for K'von, he was all of those characters and more, in one. He was the most dangerous of them all, but no one would have known that if they didn't know him.

Being president of the operation, he thought and moved like a person who ran a S & P 500 company. When he got to his office and opened the door the four of them were sitting there talking and laughing up a storm. He walked in and shook hands with all of them, then sat down at his desk.

"Let's discuss business," K'von said in a smooth voice, as if he was a Don.

One by one, each of them gave him an update report on how much money was made and how much product was left.

While in the meeting, Meechie asked K'von what he thought about him and some of his soldiers setting up shop in Iowa.

"Iowa! Who do you know in Iowa?'"

"One of the homies from the west side that I went to school with, J Roc, has been living down there for a year now—and he said it's a gold mine."

"I don't know, little bro," K'von said doubtfully.

"I see you're not opposed to it," Meechie said. "How about I go check it out for myself to see what it's like, then get back with you at a later date?"

"That's more like it. You know we don't take another man's word, we have to see if for ourselves to believe it," K'von said. "By the way, I want you guys to know that there will be a big shipment coming in next week—kilos of cocaine, pounds of weed, kilos of heroin and molly pills."

"Why so big?," Fab asked.

"My plug is going to be gone for a few months, so he decided to drop a very big load on us."

"Man, we are like a baby cartel," Fab said.

"You got that right!," Meechie said.

"What day is the shipment supposed to be coming?," Mo'tik asked.

"All I know is sometime next week, but I will let you all know as soon as I find out. Just be on point and ready to ride. Is there anything else that needs to be addressed at this time?," K'von asked them.

Each one of them said no.

"Well, this meeting is adjourned then. Are you fellas going to hang out with me tonight?," K'von asked.

"Of course," they all said.

"Call downstairs and get someone to bring us up a bottle of Cîroc," Meechie said.

K'von picked up the phone and called Big T.

"What's up, boss?"

"You got everything under control down there?"

"Boss man, you know I do. When have I ever let you down?"

"Big Man, bring me a bottle of Cîroc and 5 glasses, my brother."

"I'm on it, boss!"

When K'von got off the phone, he said "it's on the way, as we speak."

"K'von, I see that you told him to bring you 5 glasses. You're drinking tonight?," Mo'tik asked K'von.

"Yes!"

K'von was not much of a drinker, but when he did drink it was usually wine. He went into his desk drawer and pulled out a box of Cuban cigars and gave them all one and lit it for them. Just as he was about to say something he was interrupted by a knock at the door.

"Come in," he said. It was Big T, and he walked in and sat the tray down on the desk. Mo'tik cracked the top on the bottle and filled everyone's glasses. The five of them held their glasses in the air and made a toast to their success. After their toast, they sat in K'von's office talking and laughing about life in the 'hood when they were shorties. They were having a good old time. K'von just happened to look at his watch.

"Man, it almost time for the doors to open up."
Everyone started to get up out of their seats, and Moe said " Let's go down stairs and be super stars in this piece."
Just as they were about to leave K'von's office, Meechie's cell phone rang; when he saw it was John-John, he answered it.

"What's good, fam?"

"I just wanted to let you know that it's all taken care of."

"That's what I'm talking about," he said, right before hanging up the phone.

"Is everything alright?," Moe asked him.

"Yeah," he said, with a smile on his face.

"Well, I'll meet you guys downstairs in a sec, I got to make a phone call," K'von said.

While K'von was out handling his business, Precious was back at home with his three kids. Just before K'von left to go to the club, his mother went by the kids' houses to pick them up and dropped them off at his house. It was traditional for the kids to spend the night at their father's house on Saturday, because on Sunday K'von, Precious and his three children would go church with K'von's mother as a family.

After church K'von would spend the rest of the day with them doing the things that made them happy. Family was important to him, and he valued fatherhood.

He picked up the phone and called Precious' cell.

"Hey daddy," she said when she answered.

"How are things going back at the house?"

"We are having a ball. We've been playing Uno, and guess what?"

"What?," he asked her.

"Your son K'von Jr. cheats just like you do when we play UNO."

"Whatever, I do not cheat when I play UNO."

"Whatever you say."

"Where are the kids?"

"They are upstairs playing the X Box."

"Who you talking to?," a voice said in the background. It was his daughter, China.

"Your dad!"

"Can I talk to him?"

'' *You sure can,*" Precious said, and handed her the phone.

"Hey, Princess!"

"Dad, I caught K'von Jr. cheating in Uno."

"You did!"

"I sure did, Dad. And Precious said you be doing the same thing when you play."

"Do you believe that Dad would do something like that, Princess?"

"No, Dad!"

"I love you, Princess." China gave the phone back to Precious.

"I was just checking in to see how you guys were doing. Since you guy are okay, I'll see you when I get home. "

"Okay! Love you!"

"Love you too, my love," he said to his beautiful queen. As he was about to hang up the phone, he said, "don't forget to set the alarm before you go to bed."

"I won't! See you when you get home, then," she said.

Precious loved K'von's three kids as if they were hers, and they loved her too.

She'd been wanting to have some kids of her own with K'von for awhile now; about a year earlier she had been pregnant and had a miscarriage.

After K'von got off the phone talking with Precious, he left his office to go join his partners in crime. When he made his way down the stairs he began walking around and talking with the patrons, which was his normal routine. K'von was very business-oriented and he had great social skills. He wanted to make sure that the customer was satisfied with the service in his club. Everybody knew him, because most of the people were repeat customers.

When people met him for the first time, they just seemed to fall in love with his personality—especially the women, and he had plenty of them. Somehow, he has been able to keep it from getting back to Precious so far. He moved very cautiously, and he always made sure he covered his tracks. He didn't talk to other women on his main cell phone; he had another cell phone just for that. He hid his second phone with all of his side chicks' numbers in it in a secret compartment in his car.

The club was tightly packed with people from all over the Chicago area. When he walked past the dance floor, people were swaying to the music and he stopped to watch the ladies gyrate on the dance floor for a few seconds before heading over to the V.I.P section.

After making his way through the wall-to-wall packed club he finally made it to V.I.P., where his partners were popping expensive gold bottles of Ace of Spades and Patron.

"What took you so long?," Mo'tik asked

"You know I got to do my daily routine," he answered. "Checking with customers to make sure that they are happy with the service here. I think like a pimp do: 'Purse first'. The people that come in my club to party, I see them as a paycheck, and we all know what a pay check is—money. Without them, the club wouldn't be nothing."

"I hear you on that," Moe said.

K'von was all about prosperity and not popularity; but by him having so much charisma, he had both.

While they were living it up in V.I.P, more and more women were coming in there to party with them. Moe, Fab, Mo'tik and Meechie were known in the club, because they knew how to have fun.

"It's getting packed in here, so I'll get back with you guys in a minute," K'von said as he turned around and walked off.

"Love family," Fab said.

He looked at him, balled his fist up, and tapped his heart twice.

By the club being so packed, when K'von got to moving around in the club he began sweating like a scared man in court about to be sentenced to life in prison. He stopped at the bar and had one his bartenders grab a new towel from the cabinet and he wiped his forehead. *I need to take this Armani suit coat off,* he thought to himself as he wiped away the sweat.

Normally it wasn't that hot in the club even when it was packed, so he decided to investigate. He walked over to one of the air vents and put his hand up to it. It wasn't blowing at all, so he turned the switch off and on. That still didn't help, so he decided to go to the boiler room and check to see if a fuse was blown. Just as he was about to walk off a very sexy, sophisticated, dark-skinned woman caught his eye; she was dressed in a Donna Karan one-piece jumpsuit, a pair of Stilettos, and carried a Hermes Birkin bag on her arm. He had never seen her in the club before. He noticed she was talking to his waitress Felecia, and the two were carrying on as if they knew each other. When the woman walked off, he stepped to Felecia.

"Who's the lady that you were talking to?," K'von asked.

"She a friend of mine, why?"

"What's her name?"

"Vee! Do you want me to tell her anything?"

"No," he answered, and walked off to the boiler room to check the fuse box. He walked inside and turned on the light, then went to check the fuses.

When he opened the box he could see right away that a fuse was blown. He changed it out, closed the fuse box, and turned off the light.

When he got back upstairs he scanned the club over to see if he could spot Vee anywhere. The club being so packed didn't help, either. After walking around searching for her, he finally spotted her taking to some girl. He had his eyes on her and when she noticed him looking at her, he turned his head to try and play it off; but when he turned back around she was gone. He looked to the left and the right, but no Vee in sight.

All of sudden, he felt a tap on his left shoulder and turned around; it was her.

"Do you know me?," she asked.

"Why you ask me that?"

"I saw you staring at me from across the room, as if I was somebody you thought you might have known."

"Yes! I know you, your name is Vee, right?"

She gazed him with a shocked look on her face. "Yes...and how do you know my name?"

"It's my job as a club owner to know these things," he answered smoothly.

"Oh really," she said with a smile on her face. She then thought about what he'd said for a few seconds. "I know where you got my name—from Felecia, your waitress."

"You got me! Well, my name is K'von, and it's nice to meet you, Vee."

"Same here!"

The two of them began to engage in some small talk.

"What do you do for a living?," he asked her.

"I work for a law firm, over in Indiana."

"That's good! "What made you want to be a lawyer? If you don't mind me asking."

"When I was a kid my older brother was arrested for murder although he was innocent, and since my family wasn't able to afford him a lawyer, so he had to go with a public defender—you know, the one that the state provides for you," she answered. "Guess what? He was railroaded and sent to prison. He did win his case on appeal five years later, and he was set free. Ever since that happened, I told myself that I was going to law school to prevent that from happening to any of my family members ever again."

"That's an impressive story, we need more women like you in the world," K'von said.

Vee was Cuban. She was 5"8, 145 pounds with her short hair cut into a nice style, and she had amber-colored eyes; she was a very good catch. And he was not about to let her get away. He saw that her glass was getting low.

"Can I buy you a drink?"

"Sure!"

The two went to the bar and she ordered her drink. After she got it, they went up to the third floor and found a table off in the cut where they continued to talk. K'von sat there engaging her in an intelligent conversation, and listened as she basically gave him a resume of her life, which sparked a flame; he was feeling her. She wasn't the type of lady that he ran cross every day. She was a keeper, and he knew he couldn't let her get away.

K'von had messed around with all types of women: high class, middle class, hoodrats, and even home girls. Dealing with all those different types of women, he was able to study the behavior of the women he dated, and believed he was certified to be able to tell what type of woman he was talking to. K'von was a smooth operator and confident type of guy as well; he used humor and other tactics when alluring the ladies.

K'von waited for the perfect time to ask her out to breakfast.

"Not trying to sound controlling, but you and I are going out to breakfast after the club closes," he stated confidently.

"I'm okay with that," she replied.

He knew he had to get back to handling his business, so he said to her, "it was nice talking with you, but I have to go check on a few things." He paused for a few seconds and then said, "how do you feel about us exchanging numbers?"

"I'm all for it," she said.

He pulled out his phone and stored her number in it.

After exchanging phone numbers, the two went their separate ways.

He went right to the bar so that he could write her number down on a napkin. He then erased it out of his phone; just in case Precious happened to go through his cell, she wouldn't see Vee's number.

While he was at the bar writing down Vee's number he spotted Big T standing a few feet from the dance floor, and he went over to speak with him.

"Look here, I got to leave a little early tonight, so make sure the money and everything is secured, Big man."

"I got you, boss!"

As he was walking around, he ended up running into Vee again.

"Are you having fun?"

"Yes! I'm enjoying myself tonight."

He looked at his watch and it said 1:00 am.

"How about we get out of her a little early tonight, are you okay with that?"

"Sure, why not?," she said with a smile on her face.

" I have to go grab something out of my office, then I'll meet you at the front door."

"That's fine, because I have to go let my friends know I'm about to leave."

When he got to his office he grabbed what he'd come for and left right back out, on his way to meet up with Vee so they could go get something to eat.

As he came down the stairs he could see Vee standing in the doorway waiting for him. He walked up behind her.

"Let's get out of here," he said.

He opened the door for her, and she walked out. He followed behind her, headed to his S 600 Benz.

"Nice ride!," she said when saw it.

"Thanks."

Being the gentleman that he is, he opened the car door for her, knowing that it would gain him some 'cool' points.

"You are a real man," Vee said, obviously impressed. "Most guys wouldn't have done that."

"I was raised by my mother, and she taught me how to treat a woman."

He pulled out of the parking lot, headed for the freeway. He popped in his John Legend CD and went to his favorite track, *All Of Me*.

"I love this song," she said.

"So, do I!"

On the drive to a restaurant Vee began to ask him all kinds of questions.

After about twenty minutes of questioning him as if she was a prosecuting attorney and he was a star witness in a high-profile case, they pulled into the restaurant parking lot. *Saved by the bell,* he thought to himself. He didn't think she was ever going to stop asking him questions.

K'von opened up the car door for her, and the two walked inside the restaurant. The place was jam-packed, and it didn't look like there was any where for them to sit.

" Someone will be right with you," the older lady behind the counter said. "

"Okay," K'von said.

"This is a nice place," Vee said.

"Yea, it is."

While the two were talking, a waiter came walking up and said, "Come right this way", and they followed behind her.

She escorted them to their seats. About 10 minutes or so later, their waiter showed back up.

"Are you guys ready to place your order at this time?"

"I am," she said.

"So am I."

"What would like to order?", the waiter asked him.

"Ladies first," K'von said. Vee placed her order first, and then him.

"What would you guys like to drink?"

"Orange juice," he said.

"And ice tea for me."

While they were waiting their food K'von told her some jokes, which made her laugh.

"I just love your sense of humor and you are so fun to hang out with," Vee said.

"So are you!," he said." I just love people, and I believe one of the reasons men were put here is to put a smile of a woman's face."

"Listen to you, Romeo," she said.

K'von laughed.

After enjoying a meal together it was getting late, so K'von and Vee left the restaurant so that he could drop Vee off at her friend's house. When he pulled up to the house, Vee thanked him for the good time and asked him if she could see him again soon.

"Of course," he said with a big smile on his face.

"I had such a wonderful time hanging out with you," Vee proceeded to say, "I must say, I have never let my guard down this fast for any man. You know when you first approached me, I could see the confidence in you and you gave off this impressive demeanor of importance and success. I can't lie, I was attracted to that."

K'von smiled because he knew she was right; he had heard it before from other women. That's what attracted women to him. Plus, he was smooth and attractive as well.

"Thanks for the compliment," he said. "I'm just a down-to-earth person, and I try to make people around me feel comfortable."

"You made me feel comfortable too fast though," Vee said.

"It wasn't me, it was my sense of humor."

"Okay, sense of humor."

"Well, you got my number so give me a call when you are ready to hang out again."

"Now, if you call me and I don't answer right away, it's because I'm so busy.

I also own four other businesses. I maintain them, and the nightclub keeps me busy."

"You're just the perfect gentlemen aren't you, for a real woman like me. You are blessed," she said.

"You know the old saying: you reap what you sow. Plus, I was always taught that if you take care of the world, the world's going to take care of you.

So, it's just a blessing from above."

"Amen to that," Vee said.

He gave her a hug and she got out of the car. He watched her walk into her friend's house to make sure she got in safely. Once she was inside the house, he drove off. He knew it was late, but didn't know how late it was until he looked at his Gold Rolex watch; it said, 2:30 am. He knew he had to take his family to church in the morning so he hurried home. As he rolled down the highway he bobbed his head to some Rick Ross, who was one of his favorite rappers. It had him in a zone.

About 30 minutes later he was pulling into his driveway. He put the car in park and turned off the engine. He got out, closing the car door behind him. He walked up to the front door, put the key in the lock, and opened it. As soon as he stepped foot into the house he hurried over to the alarm to reset it; he didn't want to wake Precious and the kids.

He walked up the steps to his sons' room. He opened the door and the both of them were laying in bed, curled up with all their clothes on with the TV and X Box still on. They must have fallen asleep playing the game. He turned the TV and the game system off then left the room, closing the door behind him.

He walked down the hallway to his daughter China's room. He opened the door and she was laying in the bed, sound asleep.

Look at my precious little angel, he said to himself.

He walked over to her and kissed her on the forehead. She opened her eyes and when she saw it was him, she said," Daddy, I love you," in a low, sleepy tone.

"I love you too, sweetheart. Now go back to sleep, I'll talk to you in the morning."

He pulled the cover back over her body and walked out of her room on his way to his bedroom.

When he walked into the bedroom Precious was sound asleep. He undressed quietly because he didn't want to wake her. When he finished undressing, he climbed into bed. She must have felt his presence because she rolled over.

"How did everything go at the club tonight?"

"It's was a success. The club was packed with people, and they were spending money like crazy."

"That's good to hear," she whispered, and she must have been missing him, because she reached over and grabbed his penis and started stroking it.

CHAPTER 5

The next morning K'von woke up and got dressed so he could take his family to church. Even though he was in the game, he still took his family to church out of respect for his mother. He had made a promise to his mother years ago that he would go to church on Sunday with her. Since he was a man who didn't go back on his promises—at least, not so far—he had stood on the promise he made to his mother.

While he was in the bedroom Precious got dressed and checked on the kids, making sure that they were up and getting dressed to go to church; a tear rolled down K'von's face because that day was also the anniversary of his deceased daughter Kristie's death.

"K'von, me and the kids are ready," Precious said as soon as she walked into the bedroom.

He didn't want her to see him like that so he wiped the tears from his face.

"Okay, I'm dressed and ready to go, so round up the kids and I'll meet you guys in the car."

Once they were all in the car they drove to church. When they arrived, K'von's mother Rosa was waiting for them at the front door. K'von and his family piled out of the car and went inside to worship and praise God.

After church service the whole family went to K'von's mother's house to eat dinner. While they were sitting at the table eating, K'von's son Chris said, "Dad, you know today is the anniversary of my twin sister Kristie's death...I wish she was here with us; don't you, Dad?"

When Chris said that, it almost brought K'von to tears. It took everything in him to hold them back. Her death was something that he had hoped would not come up at all today; but he knew a twin brother would remember the day that his twin sister died. K'von looked at him with a sad look on his face and said, "Yes, it is, son."

"It sure is," his mother said. He had hoped that nobody would have brought it up because when she died he was away at college, and he blamed himself for not being there to save her life. After they finished eating dinner K'von and his family left his mother's house to go drop the kids off at their mother's house; they had school in the morning.

With Precious driving on the ride back home, K'von just sat quietly in the passenger's seat. Precious didn't say a word because she already knew why he was quiet. He was thinking about his daughter Kristie. Once they made it home she stopped the car, put it in park, and turned the engine off. K'von got right out of the car and went into the house without saying a word to her. She opened her door up and got out. When she walked into the house she could see him in the kitchen, but didn't know what he was doing. A few second later he came walking past her with a bottle of wine in his hand.

"I'll be in my man cave and I don't want to be disturbed," he said as he was passing.

"Okay."

She wanted to talk with him but knew that right then wasn't a good time, so she just gave him his space.

When he went into his man cave and shut the door behind him, he turned on some music. He then sat on the couch and poured himself a glass of wine. While he was alone trying to drink the pain away, Precious took it upon herself to call his mother.

"What's going on, Precious?"

"Your son, Mom Rosa."

"What he's done now?"

"He's having a moment right now about his daughter's death."

"I'm going to call him," his mother said.

"I don't think that's a good idea; when he walked past me carrying a bottle of wine in his hand, he specifically told me that he didn't want to be bothered right now."

"I'll let him vent then," his mother said. *"I know one thing for sure—we don't have to worry too much about him hurting himself, because he loves himself, his children, and his family. Plus, he has too much to live for anyway,"* his mother said.

"Amen to that!," Precious said.

"Call me if you need me," she said.

Right before they hung up, Precious said. "Don't mention to him about us having this conversation."

"Girl, you know I won't. I already know how he is." The two then said their goodbyes.

By the time they finished their phone call, K'von was on his third glass of wine. As he was thinking about his daughter, tears began to roll down his face; each drop that came rolling down represented the pain of his daughter Kristie's death. It had been 6 years since she passed, and one would think that as the years went by he would be able to deal with it a little better; but that wasn't the case with him. Every time he reflected on the times they shared together, the pain became deeper and deeper. One of the reasons for that was because he blamed himself for her death. Every time he thought about it, he asked himself the same question. *"Why wasn't I there to protect her?"*

After being in his man cave for hours, Precious decided to check on him. She knocked on the door.

"Sorry to disturb you," she said, "but I am about to go to bed...do you need me to do anything for you before I go?"

"Nah," he answered in a cold voice.

"Well...I'll see you in the morning, then."

"I love you, Precious," he said through the door.

"I love you too, K'von!"

When she made it to the bedroom she started to undress. After undressing, she took a hot shower and went to bed.

CHAPTER 6

When Precious woke up the next day, the first thing she did was go check on K'von. When she had gotten halfway down the stairs she saw him snoring on the couch, so she went back upstairs to get dressed for work.

When Precious arrived at the salon her sister Ashley was already there washing one of her client's hair. The two were having a conversation about what they had seen on the news the other night: about 10 Mafia Vice Lords being indicted by the feds for drug trafficking, which was something that Precious prayed would never happen to her man, K'von.

In the middle of the discussion Ashley's client said, "I know them men who were indicted have kids, and I feel sorry about how their absence is going to affect their lives from this point on."

Nia had just walked through the door of the salon, and she too chimed in on the conversation. While they were talking, more and more clients showed up and they also joined in on the discussion. The conversation started to get really intense for Precious, so she went into her office to clear her head.

After hearing the ladies talk about what it does to the children and family members when the men get themselves locked up, Precious began to think about K'von and how she, his children, and his family would be affected if he got himself locked up. The thought of him getting sent away to prison brought tears to her eyes. It was so hurtful, thinking about her longtime boyfriend—soon to be husband—K'von getting locked up and sent to prison. She could only imagine how the families of the 10 men indicted the other day by the feds felt. The fact of merely thinking about it brought tears to *her* eyes, so she could only imagine how their families felt.

She wiped her eyes with a napkin and picked up the phone to call K'von. He was still lying on the couch asleep and his phone woke him up.

"Uh, hello?" It was Precious, sounding cheerful as usual. "Hey babe, you sound like you just woke up."

He glanced at the clock, surprised that it said 11:00 am.

"Yeah! I was still knocked out. Where are you at?"

"I'm at the salon."

"I'm glad you woke me up because I have a meeting with my lawyers today at 11:30 am."

"Well, I love you and I'll see you when I get home," she said.

K'von laid his phone back down on the table and went upstairs to take a shower.

When he got out of the shower he proceeded to dress in a hurry, because he didn't like being late to an important meeting. It took him no more than 10 minutes to get ready, and out the door he went.

He got into his car and drove off on his way to his lawyer's office. When he walked into his lawyer's office the secretary greeted him.

"Good morning, K'von!"

"Good morning to you too, Sarah!"

"Fred and Jacob are in the conference room waiting for you."

When he walked into the conference room, both of them were sitting at the oval table.

"Sorry, I'm late," he said.

"It's alright! You're here now—that's all that matters, so let's get down to business," Jacob said. "You know, I met with a few city officials about the situation that happened in your nightclub. After reviewing the apostasy report, they decided not to hold you responsible for his death. With the amount of cocaine the deceased gentlemen had in his system, there was no way he could have consumed that much cocaine that night in your establishment in the short amount of time he was there. So, that's one thing you don't have you don't worry about anymore. As for the lawsuit, his family has filed one and they are planning on pursuing it. Fred can tell you more about the lawsuit because he has been handling that."

"Well, I did get chance to talk to the deceased gentleman father and I did get him to agree to settle out of court for $50,000 thousand at first," Fred stated. "But after doing some digging around in their background I found out that they filed Chapter 13 bankruptcy about three weeks ago, and their house is up for foreclosure right now. Once I found that out, I went back to the father and used that information as leverage. Guess what? He's willing to settle out of court for $15,000. Are you okay with that number?," Fred asked.

"I just want this to go away," K'von said. "So, I'd rather pay the $15,000 out of my pocket, because it's going to cost me more money fighting it in court."

"Since you are okay with it, I will write the man a check for $15,000 tomorrow and make sure the lawsuit is dropped," Fred said.

"Is there any other business that needs to be discussed?," Fred asked him.

"Nah, that was it." K'von said.

"Well, lunch is on you today," Fred said.

"I have no problem with treating you two old timers to lunch."

K'von got into his car and both of his lawyers rode together in Jacob's car to Thai's, a quiet, expensive restaurant which was his lawyer's favorite place to eat. While they were waiting on their food, he just listened to his lawyers talk about how much money they made in the stock market lately. Both of them were trying to convince him to invest in the stock market.

"Nah, that's not my thang," he said. "I'll just stick to what I know."

"I know one thing, you know how to make money," Fred said.

He just laughed at the money hungry old pricks.

K'von and his lawyers had a good relationship, but he and Jacob were really close because he would get his hands dirty for K'von if he had to. The two of them had other business outside of the law-firm as well. Jacob came from money, and he owned several other businesses. One of them was a storage place where K'von and his team would meet their connect to do all their drug transactions, and even store their product there as well. It was less risky, and no one would have ever thought that anything like that was going on there. Jacob didn't let Fred in on any of the personal dealings that he and K'von had going on outside the office. For that reason alone, K'von saw his lawyer Jacob as somebody he could call on.

Once their food came, the three of them sat there and ate their meal. The whole time K'von just listened to his lawyers tell corny jokes and talk about money. He laughed at the jokes only to make them feel good.

When they finishing eating, K'von got into his car and both of the lawyers got into Jacob's Jaguar and they all went their separate ways.

While K'von was in traffic, he got a call from his brother Meechie.

"What's good, Big Bro?"

"Life," K'von said. "What's going on with you?"

"Nothing much, just chilling with the fellas. The little homie Stab just got out of the Juvenile lockup today, so we are celebrating his release from bondage. The reason I called you, Big Bro, is because I need to have a face-to-face with you about something, so call me when you get some free time."

" Will do," he said, then ended the call.

As soon as Meechie hung up the phone, Stab passed him the fat blunt stuffed with some of the best Kush money can buy. He inhaled and held it for a few minutes then blew the smoke out of his nose.

"Pass the blunt," Stab said.

"Be patient, little nigga," he said right before he passed him the blunt.

Meechie had a team of young juveniles on his squad who pushed a lot of weigh for him at the high schools they attended, and they were all from the neighborhood, too. He felt that it was safe because if they got caught up, they would only go to the Juvenile Detention center or be released to their parents, depending on how severe the case was.

He never did any hand-to-hand transactions with any of the youngsters; his right-hand man C. K., whose nickname is Cold Killer, was the one who handled all that with the youngsters.

Meechie was a light-skinned dude with curly hair. He stood about 5"7, weighed about 200 pounds, and was a silent killer too. If you met him, you would have never known it. He kept a smile on his face at all times; he would crack jokes, but all this was a front, though.

Meechie was also a father of two children with his high school sweetheart, Paris; she was Black and French. She too was 5"7 with short, silky hair and her skin was flawless.

Their family lived in Orland Park in a nice condo. Meechie drove a new Range Rover, black with red leather interior and 26-inch black powder-coated fancy wheels on it. It wasn't too flashy, and he didn't drive it much either. His girl drove a silver C 250 Benz.

After being in traffic for 4 hours handling his business, K'von was driving down the highway and his phone rang. It was his connect, Hector calling him.

"What's going on, my man?"

"Just sitting here having some lunch."

"I been waiting on your call," K'von said.

"I just wanted to call you to inform you that drop is going down tonight, so keep your line open because someone will call you to let you know what time," Hector said.

"Okay! thanks for the heads up," K'von said.

"Take care," Hector said, then ended the call.

When K'von got off the phone, he called Moe, Fab, and Mo'tik to give them the heads-up about the shipment coming in later on that night. After notifying them, he called Meechie.

'When he answered the phone, he said, *"Talk to me, I'll talk back."*

"It' a go, so kept your line open," K'von said.

"Got you! Where are you at, bro?"

"I'm in traffic, Why?"

" I told you I need to talk you about something."

"Where are you, Meechie?"

"I'm back at the barber shop."

"I'm on my way, then."

About 15 minutes later K'von pulled up to the barber shop and drove around back. He dialed Meechie's number.

"I'm out back so open up the door," he said. Meechie got out of his seat to go open up the door. The two of them went

into the office to talk.

"What is it that's so important you feel the need to talk to me about?"

"I want to start my own record label," Meechie told him. When K'von heard that it was music to his ears. He thought to himself, *my... it's about time my little brother started thinking outside of the box.*

"That's what up, I'm proud of you. What are you going to call it?"

'4 Lyfe Records," he answered. "So, I need to talk to your lawyers to see if they would do the necessary paper work to get this label up and running."

"Look at my little brother making power moves! I'm really proud of you, bro."

"Thanks man, that means a lot to me. I'm just trying to follow in the footsteps of the one I look up to," Meechie said.

"I'll set up a date and time for you three to meet up to discuss this matter."

"Okay, that's sound good to me."

"Is that it?"

"Yeah, bro."

"Well, I'm out this joint—talk to you later, bro. "
Meechie unlocked and opened the door for K'von, and he slid right back out the back door and got into his luxury ride.

After he left the barber shop he parked his S 600 Benz at this parking ramp that his lawyer Jacob owned and hopped into a full-sized van, which he used to transport money and drugs.

He drove to his safe house to pick up the money to pay his connect for the last shipment, which was $1.5 million dollars. He unloaded the money into the van in a secret compartment. Once the money was put into the hidden stash compartment, K'von drove it to C&S Storage, which his lawyer Jacob owned as well. When he got there he unlocked the storage bin, lifted up the door, and drove in.

Once he was inside, he got out of the van and pulled the door back down and locked it. K'von and his connect had identical vans so when the drivers delivered the shipment they would swap out vans, which made it much easier for the both of them.

Once the switch was made, his connect's drivers would drive the money back to California to Hector. By doing it this way, no one would see his connect's drivers, and the drivers wouldn't see K'von or any of his GMO members face-to-face.

After the van was secured K'von lifted the door up, locked it back, and then he went into another storage bin where he had another car parked, got into it, and drove back to the parking ramp to get his Benz.

CHAPTER 7

Back at the salon Ashley and her friend Nia, an employee at the salon, went into the break room to talk.

Nia was a gorgeous Filipino and Jamaican woman, but she was a gold digger. She was 5"6 and weighed 150 with long, jet-black hair that came down past the middle of her back; her eyes were soft brown.

Nia was trying to set Ashley up on a blind date with her boyfriend's cousin Tray.

"What's on your mind girlfriend?," Ashley asked.

"I tried to call you several times yesterday, and I couldn't reach you."

"My phone was acting up so I had to take it in to get serviced," Ashley told her.

"The reason why I called was to see if you wanted to go on the blind date with my boyfriend L. B's cousin, Tray."

" I don't know Nia," Ashley said. "Judging from the blind dates you have set me up with in the past, I think I will pass."

"Come on girl, don't be like that! Let the past be the past. I been friends with you over seven years now, and I've seen the type of men you messed with—so girl trust me, I know he's your type," Nia explained. "He's smart, handsome, a sharp dresser, and he owns his own car lot."

"If what you said about him so far is true, he does sounds like my type. But I still have to see for myself, Nia."

"So, agree to go on the date then."

"I don't know! I been off the dating scene for about a year now."

"Girl, this is the perfect time to get back into the dating scene, then. Plus, you need to get out the house if nothing else, Ashley. So, are you going to help your girl light this city on fire, or what?"

Nia was trying her hardest to convince her best friend to go on the blind date with her boyfriend's cousin.

"I do need to get back in the dating scene," Ashley admitted, "and I have been thinking about it lately, too. Plus, I'm not getting any younger. I guess I'll go! Lord knows I could use a good laugh," Ashley said.

"That's what I'm talking about, girlfriend," Nia said. "Thank you so much sis! I owe you big time, and we'll pick you up around 9:00 tonight."

"Alright, girlfriend!"

The two had been talking for about twenty minutes and Nia finally said, "I better get back to work before your sister come in here and cuss me out."

When Nia left the room, Ashley sat in the break room and started thinking about her past relationships with men. She thought about all the men she'd loved whom she felt never loved her back; her thoughts dwelled especially on her relationship with Ricky, her last boyfriend.

After their breakup, she had been heartbroken to the point that she'd felt like a failure at love. It tore her heart into pieces every time she thought about him. It had taken her a while to get over their break up, and she couldn't believe that she'd let Nia convince her to go on a blind date.

Ashley knew she was a great catch. She was 5"10 with walnut -colored skin, long black hair that ran down to the middle of her back, and her body was bangin'. She was a 40-year-old single woman with no kids, working at a salon but also attending school to get her real estate licenses. She was well-educated, cute, and had a wonderful personality. She even worked out four day a week. The more she sat there thinking about her past relationships with men, the more upset she became; when she thought about Ricky, it just touched a nerve.

The two had been dating for about 3 years, and Ashley just knew that Ricky was the one she was going to marry. Ricky had her heart for sure; she was like a puppet on a string when it came to him. Everything had changed when she decided to pay him a surprise visit; that's the day she had found him in bed with another woman.

When Ashley had asked who the woman was, he'd said, "She's just an old acquaintance."

"That's fine...but why is she laying in your bed with just her panties and bra on?! And why is she even at your crib anyway?"

"She just came in town and I told her she could stay here since she didn't have nowhere else to go. The reason why she is laying in my bed with just her panties and bra on is...because she was on her way to take a shower, and she stopped in here to ask me a question."

Ashley wasn't buying it. So, she'd turned around and walked out the door. He had followed behind her trying to explain to her, but she wasn't trying to hear what he was saying. When they got to the front door, she had pulled it open and the door swung back and hit him in the face. The impact of the door hitting him in the face busted his nose, and it started to bleed.

He'd walked back into the bedroom where his lady friend was. "I think my nose is broken," he'd said.

"Let me see!"

When he'd opened up his hands they were all bloody, and his nose was kind of out of place. The woman ran into the bathroom, grabbed a towel, and then ran to the fridge for some ice to put it in. When she returned to the bedroom she held the towel to his nose to help with the bleeding.

After finding Ricky in bed that day with another woman, she'd decided to end it with him because she felt that she couldn't trust him, and she went on with her life.

Ashley had had enough of thinking about her past relationship with Ricky, so she got up from her chair and went back to work.

After working eight hours it was quitting time for Ashley and Nia. They grabbed their belongings and headed for the door.

"I'll see you about 9:00," Nia said to Ashley as she was leaving.

"Okay!," Ashley said.

When they got outside the two of them walked off in separate directions heading to their vehicles. Ashley got into her white Lexus ES 350 and drove off, headed to the mall to find something to wear on her blind date.

Driving down the street, she was stopped by the stop light. While she was waiting for the light to change Nia pulled up alongside her in her X5 BMW.

She honked her horn and Ashley looked to her right. Nia waved at her then turned the corner.

CHAPTER 8

On the drive to her condo after leaving the mall, Ashley thought about the blind date and couldn't stop thinking about what a bad idea it was. When she got home, she called her friend Nia.

"Girlfriend, I got cold feet and I don't think I can go on this blind date."

"It's too late for that now," Nia told her.

"Alright!," Ashley said.

"Look here, I 'm going to finish getting dressed, and I advise you to do the same," Nia said, then hung up the phone.

"Hello, hello!" Ashley said. "I know this B*tch didn't just hang up on me," she said out loud.

She laid her phone down on the counter and went into her bedroom to finish getting dressed. She was so nervous about going on this date, she had tried on about ten different outfits.

After trying on about thirteen outfits, she finally decided to wear the one that she had just bought that day at the mall. She turned around to look at the clock; it said 10 minutes after 9:00. She began to worry. *He will probably back out at the last minute*, she thought to herself.

All of sudden her phone rang; she ran over to the counter and when she saw that it was Nia, she answered it.

"Girl, we are about 5 minutes away from your condo, so be ready."

When she got off the phone, she went to the bathroom to make sure her makeup was on point. She then walked back into her bedroom and put on her black red-bottom high heels. Looking in her floor-length mirror, she said, "I look stunning!" She sprayed on some Kim Kardashian perfume and grabbed her Tommy Ford bag out of the closet.

All of a sudden, there was a knock at her front door so she went into the living room to open it; she knew it couldn't be anybody but Nia. She opened the door and Nia walked in as if she owned the place. Ashley's condo was nice. She had brown oak floors throughout the entire condo, a fire place, wet bar loaded with all the amenities, and of course, her bedroom had a balcony with a beautiful view of the lake.

"Hey girl, don't you look like you're ready to be somebody's wife," Nia said right before she took a seat on the couch.

"You look nice as well, Nia," Ashley said to her.

"Girlfriend, he's driving a new black Cadillac truck."

" Girl, that don't make him a good man, Nia."

Nia was after a man's pocket; as for Ashley, she was after a man's heart.

"Let's go," Ashley said to Nia, and they walked out the door.

When they got to the truck Nia got in the back with her man and Ashley sat in the front with her date, Tray.

" You look so amazing tonight, Ashley", he told her.

" Thank you! So do you, Tray."

Right before he pulled off, Tray turned around and said to Nia, "the way you described Ashley is far from what I see right here in front of me."

When he said that, it put a smile on Ashley's face.

" What's the plans for the night?," Ashley asked.

"If you ladies don't mind, we thought about going to Joe's Bar & Grill," Tray said, "but if you guys want to do something different, I'm okay with it, because this date is really about you ladies."

He's trying to impress me for real, Ashley thought to herself.

"I like that," Nia said.

"What about you Ashley?," Tray asked.

"I'm okay with it, too."

With music playing softly on the drive to Joe's Bar & Grill, Tray and Ashley took the opportunity to get to know one another. They were deep in conversation.

" You know you just missed the turn to Joe's Bar & Grill," L.B. said.

"Man, I'm sorry! I was so caught up in our conversation."

"I see she got you eating out of the palm of her hand already," L.B said.

"That's a good thing, then," Tray said.

Tray made a U turn and headed to Joe's Bar & Grill. They pulled up into the parking lot, and Tray turned the engine off.

"Ashley, would allow me to open your door for you?," he asked.

"Sure!"

Tray got out of the truck and walked around to the passenger's side to open up the door for Ashley. As she was getting out of the truck he said, "You can thank me with a kiss later."

After he closed the door she shot back at him, "how about I thank you with one now?"

"Are you serious?"

"No! I was just trying to show you that I have a sense of humor as well."

"I love a woman with a sense of humor," Tray said.

As they walked up to the door Nia said to L.B. "Why didn't you open the door for me?"

"Don't start, Nia. We came to have a good time, and that's what we are going to do."

The four of them walked into Joe's Bar & Grill.

"Seating for 4," Nia said to the waiter.

"Nah, we would like two separate booths, please," Tray said.

Ashley just looked at Nia when he said it. The two couples were escorted to their separate booths.

Tray and Ashley hit it right off. Ashley began to open up more and more as the night went on. The two sat there eating their meals, drinking and laughing while they enjoyed each other's company. As for Nia and L.B., they argued all during dinner because she was so upset that L.B didn't open the door for her as Tray had done for Ashley.

After they were done eating they played some pool, Ashley and Tray vs. Nia and L.B. They were on their third game of pool and it was about ten minutes before the restaurant closed, so they called it quits.

When they left the restaurant, Tray dropped Nia and L.B off first so he could get some alone time with Ashley.

"See you guys later," the both of them said as they got out of the truck.

He drove off on his way to Ashley's condo to drop her off.

"I had such a great time tonight," Ashley said. "To be honest, I was so in need of that."

"It's good to hear that, and I'm glad it was me you had that wonderful time with," Tray said. "And I look forward to having many more wonderful dates together. How about you?"

Ashley had had such an amazing time, her response was,

"I look forward to many more wonderful dates together as well," she said. "It was long overdue for me to get out of the house and have some fun."

When Tray pulled up to Ashley's condo, he walked her to her door where the two said their goodbyes with a friendly hug.

CHAPTER 9

It was a quarter to 11:00 and K'von had just gotten the call from Hector that he had been waiting for, letting him know that his shipment had been delivered.

Once K'von got the call he, Fab, Moe and Mo'tik headed to the drop off spot to secure the shipment of cocaine, Molly, heroin, and weed. As for Meechie, he and some of his goons were on security.

Once the four of them made it to drop off spot, K'von called Meechie, who was up the road with six of his goons to make sure that the shipment made it to the safe house safely. "We're leaving right now," was all he said, and then hung up. With Fab behind the wheel of the van; Moe and Mo'tik riding along with 9mm pistols; and K'von trailing in another car, they pulled out of the storage place which was right by the expressway, on their way to the safe house.

After they'd driven a few miles, Meechie and his goons jumped right behind them on the expressway, just in case they had to have a shootout with the police or anybody else trying to rob them. Meechie had some real killers on his squad who were down for wherever; for GMO, they were willing to take a bullet—or someone's life—if they had to.

Once they got close to the drop off spot, Meechie and his goons turned off. After he dropped them off, he headed over to the safe house.

By the time Meechie arrived at the safe house, Fab, Moe, Motik and K'von had already started to unload the shipment and he joined in to help.

Once the shipment was unloaded they took inventory to make sure it was all there. Once inventory was done, K'von said, "Well guys, everything seems to be here." The five of them secured the shipment, said their goodbyes, and went their separate ways.

When K'von got into his car it was 15 minutes past midnight.

Since he'd already told Precious not wait up for him because he had some important business to take care of, he got on the freeway heading to Gary, Indiana to see Vee; earlier that day, the two of them had made plans for later on that night. They had been talking back and forth on the phone since they'd met at his club. He pulled out his cell phone to call and let her know that he was on his way. When she answered she sounded wide awake.

"Hello! You must be on your way."

"Yes, I am. I was calling to make sure you were up."

"I'm wide awake."

"Alright, see you when I get there," he said, and ended the call.

When Vee got off the phone with him she went into the bathroom to freshen up; she was about to give her goods up to K'von tonight.

About forty-five minutes later he was pulling up to Vee's condo. It was nice, for a woman who was working at Moss Law Firm. He called her cell to let her know that he was outside.

"I'll be right down," she said, then hung up. She hopped out of bed and hurried down the steps because she was excited about seeing him; she opened the front door to let him in.

When he stepped inside her condo, he was surprised. It was immaculate, and everything was nice and neat. That's what he had been hoping to see anyway; if it hadn't been, he would have made up an excuse to leave. He was really impressed with everything from the furniture to the carpet; it was all upscale.

"Lovely place you have," he said.

" Thank you! It's probably nothing compared to your place. I bet your place make my place look like sh*t."
Being the humble man that he was he said, " I'll take your place over mine any day."

"Have a seat, I'll be right back," she said, walking off.
Vee was surely K'von's type of woman. He was definitely going to make her his side chick. She was a very sexy woman, very conservative, and he found those two things very attractive in a woman.

She disappeared for a few minutes, then came walking back into the living room.

"I know you're tired from being on the road, so let's go upstairs."

When he walked into her bedroom he looked around. She had a king-size bed with a lot of nice pillows on it. She had lit candles everywhere, which gave the room a sexy and sensual vibe. From observing the set up in her bedroom, he just knew some sexual pleasuring was about to take place.

"Make yourself comfortable," she said.

K'von sat on the edge of the bed and she turned on some music. The music set an erotic tone. She walked back over to the bed.

"Would you like anything to drink?," she asked.

"A glass of water," he answered.

While she was downstairs getting him some water, K'von laid across the bed listening to the music. From the vibe of the room, he just knew something was about to go down.

When she came back into the bedroom she handed him a bottle of Fiji water.

"This is my favorite kind of water," he said.

"Mine too!," she said.

"Thank you very much!"

"You're welcome."

He cracked the bottle top and took a big sip. While he was sipping, she went into the bathroom and when she returned to the bedroom she had on a pink silk robe, tied at the waist. His eyes just lit up when he saw her. To be honest, mostly sexual thoughts of her had been heavy on his mind ever since the night he'd met her at his club.

"You like?," she asked as she spun around.

"Yes, it looks gorgeous on you...it comments your skin complexion."

She looked at him with her beautiful brown eyes and started to disrobe. She dropped the robe on the floor and under it she wore a black lace bra and panties with pink ribbons. Her body was to die for. From looking at her body, K'von could tell that she worked out. He licked his lips and then exhaled; what she had on was making him break out in a sweat.

"Are you Okay?"

He took a sip of his Fiji water. "Of course!," he said. The whole time she stood there in just her bra and panties he was thinking to himself, *I'm about to give her a night that she will always remember.*

She walked over to the bed like she was a supermodel and started taking off his clothes, one article at a time, until every last article of his clothing was off.

"Do you mind if I give you a massage?," she asked.

"Not at all."

She then grabbed the bottle of massage oil and began massaging him with her soft, small hands starting with his back. After massaging his back, she worked her way down to his legs, then his feet. After she finished his feet, she asked him to roll over onto his back.

Right away she applied massage oil onto his chest.

"That feels so good," he said as she massaged his chest area.

"If you think that feels good, wait until I massage you down below."

She continued to work her way down his body. When she got to his manhood, she started massaging it with her mouth instead of her hands.

The two of them sexually pleased one another until 3:00 in the morning. When he finally made it home it was about 4:00 am, and Precious was in the bed sound asleep. He took off his shoes and laid down on the couch because he didn't want to wake up Precious because then she would have known what time he came home that night.

CHAPTER 10

When K'von woke up around 10:00 a.m. he noticed a note on the table. It was from Precious, letting him know that she would be home later and if he found time out of his busy day, she would appreciate him coming to pick her up at the salon to take her out for lunch.

He got up off the couch and went upstairs to the bathroom. He turned on the shower so he could wash the sex off him from making love to Vee the night before. Before he hopped in the shower he went into the bedroom and called Meechie.

When Meechie answered, K'von said. "I need you to call the guys and let them know that the meeting has been changed to 1 o'clock instead."

"Is everything alright family? You sound like you're sick."

"I'm Gucci! I just woke up. I was out moon lighting last night until about 4:00 in the morning."

"What did Precious have to say when you made it home?"

"I slept on the couch so I wouldn't wake her, so she doesn't even know what time I came in last night."

"You're a slick one, big bro. I see now where I get my ways from."

"Nah, don't put that off on me," K'von said then burst out laughing.

"I'll see you at 1:00," he said, and then hung up.

114

After he got off the phone he went into the bathroom to take his shower.

Even thought it was after 10 o'clock, he still felt exhausted from last night so he put his head under the shower so that the hot water could wake him up.

After taking a 30-minute shower, he got out and got dressed. Once he finished putting on his clothes he looked at the clock; it said a quarter till 11:00. He grabbed the keys to his S class Benz off the nightstand and down the stairs he went, out the front door on his way to meet Precious for lunch. He dialed her number while in traffic.

"Good morning my love," he said when she answered.

"Good morning to you too, babe."

" Can you meet me at the restaurant for lunch?"

"Yes, I can," she said with excitement in her voice. After she hung up she went to her sister Ashley and said, " I'm about to go meet K'von for lunch, I'll see you when I get back."

"Okay, and have a great lunch date with your husband-to-be."

She then went into her office, grabbed her purse, then head for the door.

He'd ended up making a stop, so about 45 minutes later K'von was pulling into the parking lot of Beef & Brandy restaurant on Jackson & State. He could see that it was packed already. Once he found a parking spot he called Precious to see how far off she was.

"Where are you at, babe?"

"I'm just pulling into the parking lot as we speak."

He looked around and when he saw her he said, "I see you now."

She parked her F Type Jaguar truck and the two of them went inside the restaurant where they were then escorted to their table.

"Someone will be coming to take your order in just a few minutes," said the lady who escorted them to their seats. While they were waiting for their server to come, they looked over the menu.

"I wish they'd hurry up because I'm starving," he said.

Soon after he said that, their server came walking up to the table.

"Hello, my name is Tiffany and I will be your server today. Are you guys ready to place your order at this time?"

"Yes, I'm starving," K'von said.

They had been to this restaurant several times, so they already knew what was on the menu. Once they placed their order, their server read it back to them to make sure she had everything right.

"That's it," Precious said.

While they were waiting for their food to come Precious asked K'von what his plans were for the rest of the evening.

"I got a meeting at 1:00 with my GMO brothers to discuss some very important business and after that I don't have any other plans. Why, you need me to be available?"

"Nah, I was just wondering because after I close the salon down, I was going to go home, take a shower and watch a movie; I was wondering if you wanted to join me."

"I would love to have movie night with my amazing girlfriend."

"It's a date, then—and don't forget, because you know how you are."

While they were discussing their plans for later that night, their server was bringing their food to the table. She placed their food on the table.

" Enjoy your meal," she said.

While they were eating, out of nowhere Precious said, "Babe, I need to run something by you to see what you think about it."

"What is it?," he asked.

"I been thinking about opening up a second Earth Beauty Salon on the south side of the city."

"How long have you been thinking about doing that?"

"For a while now," Precious answered. "And I was planning on making my sister Ashley's best friend Nia the manager."

He gave her this blank look and she just knew he was about to shoot it down.

"You know I got your back, so tell me what you need me to do make this possible."

K'von wasn't really for it, but he approved it because he was very supportive of his girl.

After they were done having lunch together K'von walked Precious to her truck. He opened the door for her and right before she got in, he grabbed her backside and squeezed it; they kissed.

While he had his arms around her kissing her, K'von looked at his watch; it said 12: 45 pm. He had pushed the meeting with his GMO brothers back once already today, and he didn't want to have to push it back any more.

"I got to go babe, I'll see you at the house later on tonight," he said, and gave her one more kiss on the lips for the road.

"Drive safe," she said to him as he was walking away.

When he got to his ride, he hopped in and shut the door behind him; he called Mo'tik.

"Let everybody know that I'm stuck in traffic and I will be there in about 20 minutes," he said.

"I'll let them know. Everybody's here but Meechie, but I just spoke with him and he said he's on his way."

"Alright. In the meantime, if you need me just hit me on my cell," K'von said.

"I'll see you when you get here, family," Mo'tik said before ending the call.

About 25 minutes or so later K'von was pulling up at the safe house, which was owned by K'von's lawyer, Jacob. It was where they'd stored a certain amount of their drugs to keep them from having to run back and forth to their main drug stash. When he walked into the safe house all four of them were sitting down at the oval table talking.

"What you guys talking about?," he asked them.

"I was telling them about the record label that I'm about to start up," Meechie said. "And Fab and Moe was telling me and Mo'tik about their clothing store that they were about to open up as well."

"Look at my brothers, being open minded about the corporate world. I'm proud of you all, and congratulations to you guys, too. If there is anything that I can do to help you, just let me know and it's done," K'von said.

"What about you, Mo'tik, you have any business ventures?," K'von asked.

"I got something in the oven, but it's not fully cooked yet...but I will put it on the table when it is done."

"Aright then let's get down to business," K'von said.
When he said that, Fab started laughing. K'von look at him.

"What's so funny, fam?"

"Look at us," Fab said. "Who ever knew that the five of us would come from the west side of Chicago—our homes, our classroom, our livelihood, and our proving grounds. A place where, most of the time all we saw was drug dealing, violence, fast money being made, pimpin' going on. A place where if you lived to see 16, it was a blessing. We saw other people being betrayed, killed, and saw tears rolling down the faces of loved ones and our friends' mothers' from losing their child at a young age.

You know we were one of the blessed ones," Fab continued. "Even though we're in the game, which we all know is not right, the blessing of it all is that we are not dead. Who would have *ever* thought the five of us would team up and do something like this on a massive scale?"

"Nobody, not even us," Moe said.

"Amen, to that," Fab said.

"Man, you going to burn in hell for saying that," Meechie said.

"Man, you will be surprised how God works," Mo'tik said. "He's an all-knowing and forgiving God. So even though we are in these streets willfully sinning, daily, he still forgives us."

"You're right," K'von said. "Enough of you sinners taking about who God is, let's get down to business."

They sat at the round talk discussing present and future GMO business. After a couple of hours of discussing, their meeting adjourned. After K'von, the GMO's CEO-street pharmacies made sure everybody's drug orders were filled Moe, Fab, Mo'tik got into their vehicles and went their separate ways.

"Be safe guys," K'von said as they were leaving.

Meechie stayed behind because he needed to speak with his brother.   "Did you speak to your lawyers about what we talked about at the barber shop a few days ago?"

"Matter of fact, I did. And they would like to meet up with you on Friday at 2:00 O'clock."

"That's not a good day for me. How about the next week some time?," Meechie asked.

"I'll tell you what, how about you tell me what time would best for you and I will pass it on to them."

"Next Friday at 10:00 O clock would be a perfect time for me."

"I'll get in touch with them to see if they could see you on that day at that time," K'von said.

"Thanks, big bro, you are the best," Meechie said. "Bro, do you remember when we were in your office at the club and I was telling you what my man's J Roc said about Iowa? That it was a gold mine? Well, me and some of my guys are about to shoot down there for about a week or so to check thing out."

"Who's going to take over your day-to-day operations here while you're gone?"

"My second-in-command and close friend, Law," Meechie answered.

"I like Law...he a solid dude, and he has a great business mindset as well. I know he will hold things down while you are gone."

Out of nowhere, Meechie then said, "I got a favor to ask of you. Bro, hear me out first before you say anything...I know you don't like doing this, but I need 3 kilos of cocaine, and some mollies to take down there with me along with some weed."

"You know I wouldn't normally approve of this; but I will make an exception this time, because you're taking it out of town—so you are really not stepping on Moe or Fab's toes," K'von said. "Plus, I consider this an economical move to expand the empire."

"Thanks bro, you won't regret it," Meechie assured him. "My man J Roc is already established down there, and he's going to be the one who push the product for me. The fact that his cash flow will not let him buy enough product to keep up with the demand down there made me decide to go help him out with that," Meechie said.

After he gave Meechie the approval K'von walked over to the kilos of cocaine and grabbed three of them, a 500-pack of mollies, and 100 pounds of kush weed. The two locked the place up, then said their goodbyes because K'von had to meet up with a friend of his.

CHAPTER 11

Back at the salon, Nia was showing signs of jealousy because of the roses that Tray had delivered to Ashley at her job.

"Look at you girl, you think you're all that because you got some flowers," Nia said.

"What are you talking about?" These flowers don't mean nothing to me. Yes, it was nice to have received flowers from him, but it's not going to my head."

"Girlfriend, you know I'm just messing with you."

Deep down inside, Ashley felt Nia was jealous of her getting flowers. She thought about the comment Nia had made to L.B the night when the four of them were on a date, about Tray opening the door for Ashley and L.B didn't for her.

Nia then changed subjects. "Girl, give me all the juicy details that happened after he dropped you off. "

"There's no juicy details to tell. When we got to my condo, he walked me to the door and we hugged; that was it," Ashley said.

"Girl, I talked to L.B this morning and he said Tray really likes you. Are you going to go on more dates with him?"

"I don't know."

"Girl if I was you, I would milk him for all that I can until he decides to move on to the next woman," Nia said.

"Girl, you are nothing but a gold digger, Nia! I don't have time for this, I got to get back to work," Ashley said, then walked off.

K'von had just left the safe house; he was on his way to meet up with a friend to talk business when his cell phone rang. When he saw that it was his older sister Tasha calling, he hurried and answered it.

"Mom is in the hospital," she said as soon as he picked up.

"What happened?"

"One of the paramedics said it might be a heart attack, he doesn't know for sure."

"What hospital is she at?"

"She's at Mercy."

"I'm on my way," he said, and hung up.

After he hung up with his sister he called Meechie, but all he got was his voice mail. He then called Precious.

"My mom is in the hospital," he said as soon as she answered.

"What happened?"

"Tasha said something about a heart attack. We really won't know what's going on until she sees the doctor."

"I'll say a prayer for her," Precious said. *"Do you need me to meet you there?"*

"Just take care of the salon and I will call you as soon as I hear something."

"I love you baby," she said.

"I love you too!"

On the way to the hospital all K'von could think about was losing his mother, which was something he had never, ever thought about.

K'von and his mother were so close; she wasn't just his mother, she was also his best friend. It would hurt him if something bad happened to her. She wasn't just his mother, she was also his best friend. So, he lifted his mother up in prayer. *"Please God let her live. I need her here with me,"* he said out loud as he was riding down the freeway.

30 minutes later he pulled into the hospital parking lot. He looked for a parking space, and he when he found one he hurried up and parked his car. He swung the door open and ran into the emergency room. He asked the lady at the front desk what room Rosa Scott was in.

She looked at her chart and said "room 201", and K'von took off running before she could give him directions to his mother's room.

He pushed the button on the elevator and when it opened he got on. It stopped at the second floor and he hopped off in a hurry. He saw a nurse walking past, and he stopped her.

"Can you tell me where room 201 is?"

"Yes, follow me, I'll take you right to it."

He followed behind her, breathing like he was about to have a panic attack.

When he walked into the room for the first time, seeing his mother hooked up to a machine with tubes all in her body scared him; she was lying in the bed with her eyes closed, looking as if she were dead. The doctor was writing in the chart as he was examining her. K'von walked over to the doctor and said, "Doc is she going to live? I can't lose my mother."

"Son, calm down...everything will be alright", the doctor said to him. "We think it might be just a mild stroke, but we won't know until her lab results get back."

After the doctor left the room K'von walked over to his mother's bed and kissed her on the forehead. "I love you mom," he whispered to her.

"I love you too, son," she said softly.

After hearing her voice, he cheered up just a little. "Mom, everything is going to be alright," he assured her. "I said a prayer for you on the way to the hospital. I asked God to watch over you."

"That was so loving of you, son. You know God is the only one we can fully trust with our lives. And if you said the prayer with faith, he will answer it because whatsoever ye ask for when ye pray, if he believes that ye shall receive it!"

K'von and Tasha sat in the room with their mother, talking and waiting for the doctor to come back in the room to let them know the lab results. K'von had noticed that the right side of his mother's neck was swollen.

"Mom, when you get out of the hospital I want you to come stay at my house for at least a couple of weeks."

"Son, I'll be fine at my own house."

K'von's mother and sister Tasha sat in the room talking and listening to K'von crack jokes. His mother just sat there and smiled. K'von loved to put a smile on his mother's face. She had a smile that would just melt your heart. About an hour or so later, the doctor came back in the room.

"Good to see that you're in good spirits, Mrs. Scott. You have a beautiful smile," he said to her. "Well, your lab results just came back and everything looks normal," the doctor stated. "But I want you to keep an eye on that swelling on the right side of your neck. If it doesn't go down in a few days, I suggest that you go see your doctor. You're free to go," he said.

"Thanks for everything Doc," K'von said.

"Thank *you* for thanking *me*. It's my job to do whatever needs to be done to save a life." He then pulled K'von off to the side and said, "keep an eye on her for the next couple of days at least."

"Will do, Doc." K'von shook his hand.

K'von left the room and Rosa went into the restroom to get dressed. Then K'von, Tasha and their mother headed toward the front entrance. K'von opened the car door for his mother. He then helped her into the car and closed the car door. He hugged his sister, and she got into her car and drove off.

Tasha drove her to her house, because she and K'von had decided that was where their mother needed to be so that someone could keep an eye on her.

K'von checked his phone when he got into his car; he'd left it in there because he was in such hurry. He called Precious just to let her know that his mother was okay. When she answered, she said, *"please tell me everything is alright."*

'Yes, she is fine. She was just released about 5 minutes ago."

"That's good to hear, because I was over here stressing. I love you, babe!," Precious said.

"I love you too, I'll see you when I get home tonight."

After he got off the phone with Precious, he called the friend whom he'd been on his way to see before receiving the phone call from Tasha telling him that their mother was in the hospital. K'von was now back in traffic.

Being a concerned son, he picked up his cell and called his mother to checkup on her while on the way back from seeing his friend. His sister Tasha answered the phone.

"How's mom doing?," he asked.

"She's seems to be doing much better. She's taking a shower right now. Is there anything that you want me to tell her when she gets out?"

"Just let her know that I called to checkup on her, and that I love her."

"Will do, big bro."

It was now 9:00, and he pulled into Walgreen's, where he went inside to buy some Mike- n- Ike, Sour Patch, and a box of Dove chocolates, some of his girl Precious' favorites. After he found everything that he was looking for he went to the counter, paid for the items, and left. He got back into his car and headed home. It was about 10:00 when he finally made it. When he pulled into the driveway, he could see Precious' F Type Jaguar truck sitting in their long driveway. He turned off the engine and went inside. As soon as he came walking through the door he called her name. When he got no response, he called her name a second time; still, no response.

He headed up the stairs, thinking that she might be in the shower. When he walked into bedroom he could hear the water running. He walked into the bathroom and there she was, taking a shower. He opened the door.

"Can I join you?," he asked.

"Yes, you can," she said with a smile on her face.

He took off his clothes and got into the shower with her. When the hot water hit him, he said, "I need this after the exhausting day I've had."

While they were in the shower Meechie was calling him back, because he'd left a message on his cell phone earlier telling him to call him because it an emergency.

When he got out of the shower he checked his phone and saw that he had about 5 missed calls from Meechie. He called him back.

"What's the emergency?," Meechie said.

"Mom had to be rushed to the hospital by ambulance."

"Is she okay? I'm on my way back."

"She's fine, it wasn't nothing serious. She just needs to get some rest, that's all."

"I'll call you in the morning, I'm about to call and check up on her," Meechie said.

When he got off the phone, he turned around. Precious was wearing all black, lace, one-piece lingerie that was to die for.

"My love, you look so beautiful in that one-piece," he said. She grabbed the matching silk robe and put it on.

"You can't have this until we're done watching the movie," she said.

He finished getting dressed and the two of them went into their home movie theater to watch season four of "Power"—which was their favorite movie—K'von thought he was Ghost in real life, and Precious thought she was Ghost's wife Tasha in real life. When the movie ended, the two went into their bedroom to have some sexual fun.

CHAPTER 12

Meechie, Roc, and Bub drove up to Waterloo, aka 'the City of No Love' to see his boy J Roc, who'd been running drugs out of the Carter building projects on Allen and 1st Ave. The first night in town J Roc and his boys took Meechie, Roc and Bud to a strip club called the Juice Bar.

Meechie hadn't been in town more than three hours and he was already getting off track from his original game plan, which was to come to Waterloo to see if it was worth setting up shop.

In no time, he went from peeking the scene to see if it was a lucrative business investment to peeking out the ladies in the strip club.

When they walked through the front door of the strip club, DJ Fret gave them a shout out; he knew J Roc and his guys to be regulars at the club.

"Baller alert, J Roc's in the house and he brought a team of other ballers with him!" only attracted attention to Meechie, who was supposed to be in town for only one reason—to see if the city of no love was worth investing in.

Now, all eyes were on them; the strippers that were working that night flocked right to them.

These guys were 20-deep in the V.I.P section popping bottles of Belaire and Remy, drawing attention to themselves. Their splurging caught the attention of a few local stick-up boys.

Base, and his partner in crime, Mack 10 had placed strippers in the club to help them step up their robbery sting; they didn't like out-of-towners coming into their city unannounced. They sent Moo'ca, one of their dancers that they had working the club that night to go join them in the V.I.P to see what she could find out. Meechie, Bud and Roc were the three that they focused on, because they already knew who J Roc and his boys were.

Once they were full of liquor, they began to turn up. They were spending money on lap dances and making it rain on strippers while they were performing on stage. They popped bottle after bottle until the strip club closed, and Moo'ca was right there the whole time, in Meechie's ear. It was about closing time, and Meechie and Moo'ca were in the cut talking when Mack 10 had Ebony, another one of their strippers, go join them. He knew that men's weakness was women. While Meechie and Moo'ca were talking, Ebony came rolling up.

"Moo'ca what's your plans after the club closes?," she asked.

"She coming with me, why?" Meechie said. " What's your name?"

"Hi, I'm Ebony!" She reached out her hand and he shook it.

"Nice to meet you, Ebony."

Meechie liked what he saw.

"What are *your* plans after you leave the club?," he asked Ebony.

"I would like to hangout out with you guys, if you don't mind."

"Of course not. Do you mind if Ebony joins us?," he asked Moo'ca.

"That's my girl, the more the better," Moo'ca said.

Meechie gave Moo'ca the address to J Roc's crib.

After partying at the strip club for hours, popping bottles of champagne and Remy, Meechie and his guys were sloppy drunk. They headed over to I HOP for something to eat to help soak up some of the liquor that they had been drinking all night long.

When Meechie made it to the car he said, "I'm about to have a threesome tonight."

"With those two strippers I seen you talking to by the bar?," Roc asked.

"You know it!"

On the way to I HOP the fellas were discussing the fun they'd had at the strip club, and who they were going to bang after they were done eating.

While they were at I HOP eating, their cell phones were ringing off the hook; it had gotten so bad that they just took their meals to go.

"Let's shake this spot so we can go have some fun with these strippers we met at the club," Meechie said. So, they all piled into their vehicles and headed back to J Roc's place to meet up the strippers. J Roc had a six-bedroom house with a finished basement on Locust Street.

When they pulled up to his crib, some of the strippers were already at the house waiting in their cars.

"How did they know to meet us here?," J Roc asked.

"I gave a few chicks that I was planning on hooking up with your address, and I told them to bring some friends too," Meechie said.

"So, did I," Bud said.

As they all piled out of their vehicles and into the house, J Roc wasted no time in getting the party started. He fired up some Kush, poured some molly pills on the table and brought out some Hennessey to drink.

Meechie just sat on the couch with Moo'ca and Ebony watching it all go down. After the liquor, the weed and mollies started to kick in; the ladies' clothes came off and they walked around the house butt-ass naked.

J Roc ducked off into his room and when he came walking back into the living room, he had a box filled with condoms. He poured them on the table.

"Make sure you guys practice safe sex."

People started having sex right there in the living room, going from one sexual partner to the next. It was just one big old orgy going on.

While all this was taking place, Meechie pulled out a blunt and started to pack it with some of the finest weed that money could buy. Once he'd finished packing the blunt with weed, he rolled it then licked the cigar paper to seal it. He then lit the blunt and took a puff. When he was done smoking the blunt Ebony and Moo'ca stood up, and Meechie grabbed both of them by their hands and off to the bedroom they went to have some fun.

When they walked into the bedroom, he slammed the door behind him and Ebony locked it. The girls didn't waste any time getting the sexual party cracking. They started kissing on each other, and the whole time this was going on Meechie just sat in the chair smiling like the boss he was. After kissing on each other the two women had enough and they wanted to get more intimate, so they stripped down to nothing. Moo'ca laid on her back while Ebony made her way town to her intimate area.

While they were going at it, Meechie was thinking to himself, *this is going to be one heck of a 'welcoming to our city'.* Then the two started giving each other lengthy kisses and Ebony stopped and asked Meechie, "Why don't you come over here and join us.".
He'd had enough so he started to get undressed. Then he reached into his pants pocket, pulled out a condom, then Ebony put it on him and the three of them began to have a threesome.

While Meechie was in 'the city of no love' making love to two strippers he'd met at the strip club, one of his soldiers back in the Chi named Smoke G was being robbed. The three intruders came into his crib while he and his girl Azia were lying in the bed asleep.

He was awakened by being slapped upside his head with a pistol. When he saw the intruders standing over him pointing their guns at him, all he could think was, *'they caught me slipping'*.

"Get up," one of the intruders said to his girl. She woke up and saw him pointing a pistol at her, and she froze up.

"This is a robbery, so don't make it a homicide," one of the intruders said out loud. "So where is the money?"

"What money? " Smoke G said.

"You think I'm stupid," the intruder said, then cracked Smoke G on the bridge of his nose with the butt of his gun.

"Fuck!," he said.

"Now, are you going to cooperate?"

By then, one of the men was standing at the bedroom door; one had his gun pointed at Smoke G, and other had his pointed at Smoke G's girlfriend.

"Take me to the money," said the taller, muscular intruder of the three who had his gun pointed at Smoke G. "And if you don't, I'm going to put bullet in your girl's head."

"There is no money here! I swear!"

"You're lying," the man by the bedroom door said.

"I've had enough," said the short, fat intruder guarding the door. He walked over to Smoke G's girl and told her to open her mouth. She started crying.

"I said, open your mouth!," and then he put his 9mm Glock inside it, hoping that this would get Smoke G to talk.

"Now, nigga keep playing with us and watch me blow your girl's brains out."

"Okay," Smoke G said. He was pulled off the bed onto the floor. Then the man pulled him up off the floor by the back of his Tee shirt.

"Now take me to the money." He walked behind Smoke G with his gun pressed into his back. When they got to the safe, Smoke G was shaking because he was scared.

"Hurry up, I don't have all day," the robber said; he pressed the barrel of the gun harder on his back. When Smoke G finally opened the safe, the intruder couldn't believe his eyes. There were stacks on top of stacks in the safe, and weed. "We hit a lick," the robber said, as he walked Smoke G to the safe with his pistol pressed into his back. Once they had emptied the money out of the safe, Smoke G and his girl were told to lie down face first on the bed.

"If I see you looking back I'm going to kill your girl, and I'm not playing!," one of the intruders said. The three left out of Smoke G's crib in a hurry.

When they heard the door shut Smoke G grabbed his gun and ran down the steps, but they were gone. He then grabbed his cell phone and called his boy C.K.

"Why are you calling me this late, fam?"

"I just been robbed."

"I'm on my way", he said, and hung up. He got dressed and headed over to Smoke G's.

When C.K. got there, Smoke G was lying on the couch and his girl was holding a towel on his nose with ice in it to try and stop the bleeding.

"Fam, did you recognize any of their voices?," C.K. asked.

"Nah," he said.

"Don't worry, well find out who they were sooner than later."

They talked for a few minutes, and then C.K rolled up a blunt and the two of them smoked it.

CHAPTER 13

The next day, everybody but Meechie was hung over. When he got up out of bed he went right into J Roc's room and woke him up. "Get up, it's time to chase this paper."

J Roc got out of bed, and he and Meechie went into one of the bedrooms to package up the drugs while everybody else was sleep. While the two of them were going into the room, Juice was coming out of the bathroom.

"Juice, make sure don't nobody come up these stairs," Meechie said.

"I got you, fam!"

After they were done packing up the product, J' Roc put them in a secret compartment that his uncle from Chicago had built when he came to visit last year.

"Who all know about your secret compartment?," Meechie asked him.

Meechie wanted to know just in case his product came up missing; he'd know who-all to drive down on about his shit.

"Nobody but me, Fam! I trust my guys, but not enough to let them know about my secret compartment."

"Are you ready to get this money?," Meechie asked.

"I'm from a city where hustlers are born and not sworn...what do you think?," J Roc said.

While J Roc and Meechie were talking, J Roc's cell phone rang.

He looked at it. "This is Tone, one of my main customers calling me right now," J Roc said.

Meechie didn't know what the guy on the other end of the phone was saying, but when J Roc got off of the phone he said, "My man wants 30 pounds of Kush and a half of slab."

"You shittin me!," Meechie said.

J Roc grabbed the half of slab, 30 pounds of Kush, then he and Meechie went downstairs. When he got downstairs J Roc saw Ike sitting on the couch.

"Come take a ride with me to the East side, solider," J Roc said.

Ike got up off the couch, grabbed his pistol, and tucked it in his waist band. "Let's go," he said.

The West and East sides don't really get along like that, so Ike had to make sure he was strapped with that tool, for sho. He and J Roc went out the door headed over to Tone's crib.

When they got close to Tone's crib, J Roc called him on the phone.

"I'm not that far away, so be on the lookout for me."

"*I will!*"

"Look here Ike, we're about to go into Crips territory so be ready to bust that tool, just in case somebody try to pull a jack move," J' Roc said to him.

Ike reached into his waistband and pulled out a chrome 44; he laid it on the front seat of the car.

"If anyone try anything, I will fill their body up with these 44 shells."

J Roc took a right, turning to the alley which led to Tone's back yard. While they were driving down the alley Ike was scoping out the scene to see if anything looked suspicious. As soon as the pulled into the back yard, Tone was looking out the window and he came right out. He hopped in the back seat and J Roc told him it was under the seat. He smelled the Kush and looked at the half of slab.

He passed J Roc the money in a paper bag.

"I don't have to count it do I?"

"Nah, It's all there! You know me better than that. I wouldn't short change you because I know it would be hell to pay," Tone said as he got out of the car and closed the door. J Roc backed the car up and drove off.

"Bro, I don't like the way he looked at me when he got in the car," Ike said.

"Bro, he just ugly as hell...that's just his normal look," J' Roc said.

Ike busted out laughing. "You're right, he is an ugly mothafucka, fam."

Even though J Roc had been doing business with Tone for years, he still didn't trust him.

"Count that paper to make sure it's all there," J Roc said to Ike.

Ike opened up the paper bag and started to count the cash to make sure the count was right. While he was counting, J Roc called back to the crib to see if anybody was hungry.

Ali answered the phone. "Ask the guys if they want something to eat from Wendy's," J Roc said.

He could hear Ali's loud mouth ass in the background yelling, *"Fellas, J Roc on the phone and want to know if you guys want him to bring you something back from Wendy's?"*

When Ali got back on the phone he told J Roc what everybody said they wanted.

"Man, tell them niggas that I can't remember all that shit. I'm just going to bring back all kind of shit off the dollar menu."

"I don't think them niggas really care what you bring back they'll eat whatever it is that you get, they just hungry," Ali said right before he ended the call.

When they pulled into the drive thru a lady's voice came over the intercom.

"Welcome to Wendy's, can I take your order, please?"

J Roc just started ordering all kinds of food off of the dollar menu.

"I would like 30 junior cheeseburgers, 30 six-piece nuggets, 30 medium fries, and 30 spicy chicken sandwiches."

"Is that all, sir? If so, can I get you to pull around to the drive thru window," the lady said.

As they were pulling around to the drive thru, Ike was still counting the money.

Put that shit away," J Roc said, so Ike covered the money up with his white tee shirt.

When they got to the drive thru window he paid the lady for the food and then drove off.

On the ride back to J Roc's crib Ike had finishing counting the money and said, "It's all here."

"Are you sure?"

"Yes, I'm sure," Ike said.

"You know your ass can't count that good, motherfucker."

"Whatever. My counting skills is better than yours," Ike said.

"Look here bro, I just want to take the time to say thank you, J Roc, for everything that you ever done for me and my family," Ike said.

"You're welcome, fam! It's nothing, fam—this is just how I was seasoned back in the Chi, growing up as a kid. Plus, you have extended the same love to me and more. I must say, that's some real nigga's shit, Ike. Nowadays, niggas are too prideful to let a nigga know that they appreciate them—as if it makes them look weak to say 'thank you' every now and then," J Roc said as he was pulling into the driveway. He parked the car and they got out and went into the house.

"The food is here," Ali said when he saw them coming through the door. Everybody came running, grabbing shit off the table. The guys hit those bags like a pack of hungry wolves.

"Hold on guys, let Meechie get what he wants first, "J Roc said.

Standing nearby, Meechie said, "I'm good they can go 'head, I'll get whatever's left over. I'm really not that hungry."

The reason Meechie did that was because he didn't want J Roc's guys to feel some type of way about him going first; he knew how petty niggas could get over the smallest thing. The guys hit those bags like a pack of wolves. There was plenty of food left after everybody got theirs, so Meechie grabbed three chicken sandwiches and some fries.

While they were all in the living room eating, J Roc said, "Yo, Ike since you're the closest could you grab something to drink out of the fridge?"

"I can do that for you," he said, and walked into the kitchen to get some 2-liters of soda from the refrigerator.

After they were done devouring their Wendy's, Meechie said, " You know what time it is: smoke time. Roll up some of the Chi town kush, Ike."

Ike rolled about ten blunts and the fellas started passing them around the room.

"Hold on, my phone is ringing," J Roc said, then stepped out of the room so that he could have some privacy. It was his boy Aki. Aki was dark-skinned and stood about 6 foot; he weighed about a hundred pounds soaking wet. He was a Boss Pimp gangster from the Chi, and he had been living in Waterloo, aka the city of no love for about six months. One thing was sure: he was a vicious killer who rarely showed his emotions.

"What's pumpin, Aki?"

Aki was a Boss pimp gangster from the Chi, and he had been living in Waterloo for about 6 months now.

Aki was tall and dark-skinned, and he wore a low cut with a fade. He stood about 6 feet, and weighed about one hundred pounds soaking wet; but one thing for sure was that he was a vicious killer. Another thing was certain: while he was smiling, he was plotting his revenge on you.

"I just called to invite you and your guys to my barbeque at 3:00."

"We'll slide thru there fam, for sure. "One love, gangster," J Roc said before he hung up his phone.

Even though J Roc was Conservative Vice Lords that didn't matter, because Aki was still from the Chi. J Roc looked past what set he claimed, because he and some of the other cats from the Chi had made a pact: while they were in the city of no love, it wasn't about the set you claimed—it was all about the city they were from.

"We have been invited to one of the guys from the crib barbecue at 3:00," J Roc said after he got off the phone. "You guys want to go?"

"I'm with it," they all said.

"How well do you know this Aki fella?," Meechie asked.

"I know Aki well. He's a Boss Pimp gangster from the city."

"I been knowing you for a long time. If you say he's cool, me and my guys are there," Meechie said.

Up until they went to the barbecue, people kept hitting up J Roc's line and he kept serving them with that Chi town cocaine, weed, and molly. He chased that paper all day until it was time to go to Aki's cookout, hoping that Meechie would be impressed and decide to set up shop in Waterloo—aka the city of no love.

CHAPTER 14

At the salon back in Chicago, aka Chi Raq, there was a little tension between Nia and Ashley. It was nothing serious, though; Ashley sensed that her best friend Nia was getting jealous of her and Tray's relationship. While the two were talking, Ashley said, "I like Tray, Nia."

"Girl, you guys only one been going out for a few weeks now, how can you let something like that come out of your mouth?," Nia said. "If you like him, you need to take your time with him or you will run him off."

"You don't know what you're talking about," Ashley said. "He's pressing up on me more than I am on him. Look here, Nia—I know you're concerned about me, but let me do 'me'. "

"The last time you did 'you', you got your heart torn into a million pieces," Nia answered. "I tried to tell you about Ricky."

Ashley knew she was right, but that was the past. Plus, it was too late; she was already attached to Tray. He has been such a gentleman to her. He sent her roses and he called her throughout the day several times to check up on her, which was something she hadn't had from a man in long time.

The fact that she has been out of the dating scene for about a year, and Tray was making her feel so special by the way he was treating her made her fall head-over-heels in love with him so fast.

"Don't get me wrong Ashley, he is a nice guy and all, but I don't trust him," Nia said.

Ashley just twisted her lips. " If you didn't trust him, why did you ask me to go on a date with him?"

"I was being selfish, and I didn't know that you were going to actually fall for him."

Ashley had had enough of Nia's jealousy and she snapped.

"Let's drop this conversation," Ashley said, "before I say something that I regret."

"Fine then," Nia said and walked out of the break room.

When she left, Ashley began to reflect again on how Nia was showing signs of jealousy on their date that night; like when Tray had opened the door for her, and Nia had asked L.B. *"Why didn't you open the door for me?"* Nia had always been jealous of Ashley, and people used to ask her why she even put up with her. Ashley saw the good in Nia, because she wasn't like everyone else—always looking at the bad and not the good inside a person.

While she was sitting in the break room, her sister Precious came in.

"What's going on with you and Nia?," she asked.

"Why'd you ask that, sis?"

"When she came out of the break room, she looked as if she was upset about something."

"She's just mad because I told her to mind her business when it comes to my relationship with Tray," Ashley answered.

"You're seeing some guy now?," Precious asked her.

"Yes!"

"Good for you, sis," Precious said. "Tell me all about him."

"He's sweet, kind and considerate. He makes me laugh, he's outgoing and handsome. And he owns a car lot, too."

"He sounds like a winner," she said.

"I feel the same way you do—but Nia, on the other hand, doesn't."

"Look here sis, follow your heart because it won't steer you wrong."

"I miss talking to you about life and relationships," Ashley said.

"I'm just a phone call away if you need to talk to me," Precious said. "By the way, your 2:00 O'clock appointment is here already."

"Let me go make this money, then." She got up out of her chair and walked to the door. Right before she opened it, she looked back and said, "Thanks for that wonderful advice, big sis."

When Ashley was done talking with her big sister, she went back to work.

"Can I talk to you, Ashley?," Nia asked.

Nia knew that her friend Ashley was upset with her; she didn't want to lose her as a friend, so she apologized to her.

"Ashley, I'm so sorry for the way that I been acting toward you. I got a lot going on in my life right now, and I hope that you forgive me for the way I been acting."

Ashley was a level-headed, loving friend and immediately said, "Yes, I forgive you!" The two hugged it out and then went back to work.

CHAPTER 15

Back in Waterloo, aka the city of no love, it was 3:30 in the afternoon; J Roc and the fellas were in traffic on their way to Aki's barbecue. When they arrived, they saw police putting up yellow tape across what looked like a crime scene. There was a female sitting on the curb, crying her heart out.

"What happened?," J Roc asked her.

"Aki just shot and killed my cousin!," she cried. Just as he was about to ask her something else, his cell rang. It was a female he was messing around with named Ivy, so he answered the phone.

"What's going on, baby girl?"

"Your boy Aki is crazy!"

"What did he do?"

"He just walked up on Sam Bo, pulled his pistol out and aimed it directly at his heart! He shot him once in the chest and once in the head, right in front of about a hundred people!"

"For what?"

"He got word that Sam Bo was the one who broke into his girl's crib and stole a kilo of cocaine from him."

After hearing that, he said, "I'll talk with you later," and ended the call.

After he got off of the phone he said, "Let's go fellas."

They all got back into their rides and headed back to J Roc's crib.

On the drive back to back to J Roc's, the fellas were getting phone calls from people telling them how it all went down. When they got back to the house they discussed what they had heard about what took place at Aki's barbecue. While discussing the incident that took place at the barbecue they didn't get to attend, this dude named Truck hit J Roc's line. When J Roc got off the phone, he said, "I got to go chase this money," and left out the door. While J Roc was in traffic making drug moves, the fellas were talking shit, and playing X Box. Meechie had watched J' Roc and some of the guys dump cocaine, Molly, and Weed all day long, like it was nothing.   Later on that day, Meechie and J Roc were in the living room sipping on some Remy Martin.

"Man, you were right about this little town, it is a gold mine, " Meechie said to him.

"I told you, family," J Roc said. "This little town is the land of milk and honey, fam. Why do you think I'm still here? It's plenty of money to be made in this city, but the problem is there is no major supplier living in the city like it is in the Chi. Now that's where you come in. You set up shop and have those kilos of cocaine and weed on deck; I believe that these cats in this town who be selling kilos and major weight will come cop their weight from you instead of going somewhere else to get it. I sell weight, but I don't have

152

enough money to buy the product that I need to meet these cats' demands here."

J Roc had Meechie's attention for real. What he was saying got Meechie's wheels turning; he had already made up his mind to set up shop in the city of no love, but he hasn't told J Roc just yet.

"Say I agree to partner with you, let me asked you this: do you mind if I bring some of the west side goons with me?"

"Not at all," J Roc replied.

'It's a go then," Meechie said. The two of them shook on it.

"If we're going to come back and take over the town, we need a name," Bud said.

"I like where you are going with this," Meechie said. "I'm cool with it...what about you, J Roc?"

"I'm with you on that," he said.

"Let's discuss names then," Meechie said.

Meechie, J Roc, Bud and Roc sat in the kitchen thinking of names. 'Chi Town Players' was the first name that came up. After discussing names for about 30 minutes, Meechie said, "I got it."

"What did you come up with?," Bud asked.

"WMF, West side Mafia Family," he said.

"I like that one, fam," J Roc said.

After being in Waterloo for a week, J Roc had sold the three kilos of cocaine, 500 hundred mollies, and 100 pounds of Kush weed that Meechie had brought with him—and people were *still* hitting up J Roc's line. Being that Meechie didn't like to leave any money on the table he, Bud, and Roc headed back down highway 80 to the Chi to go re-up. When they arrived back home to the city Meechie went to the safe house to re-up. Since he had some important business to attend back home, he sent Roc and Bud back to the city of no love with the work.

CHAPTER 16

Back in Chicago, aka ChiRaq, K'von woke up early and went into the bathroom to shower so he could dress and go handle his street life business in those streets. Precious came into the bathroom and got into the shower with him. They took a 30-minute shower together. When they got out, Precious said, "Could you dry my back off?"

K'von took the Versace towel and dried off her back. After he had finished, she walked her naked self right into the bedroom. Her backside just jiggled with each step that she took. K'von stood there in the doorway, just looking with his mouth wide open.

She grabbed a pair of underwear as she was about to put them on. After seeing her naked got his sex drive on ten, and he was wanting to get it in before heading out for the day. Just as Precious was about to pull her panties up K'von said, "Can we get a quickie in before we leave the house?"

" I got a client who I'm supposed to meet in about thirty minutes," she said. "Plus, it's going to take you all day to get yours off, so the answer is no."

"I see how you is," he said.

She knew he was upset; she walked over to him and gave him a kiss.

"I promise I will make it up to you tonight," she said in her sexy bedroom voice.

After putting on her panties and bra she walked into her walk-in closet and found an outfit to wear. She then proceeded to get dressed. Once she was finished, she walked over to the long mirror. She grabbed her Gucci purse and looked at K'von. "I look good, don't I baby?," she said to her man.

" You look like a Queen, my love."

"Don't forget that you promised that you would take me to the Bulls vs. Miami game tonight."

"I'm glad you reminded me, because I had forgot all about it. What time is the game?," he asked her.

"It at 7 o'clock".

"I'll make sure I'm back at the house no later than 6 o'clock, which will give us plenty of time to get there."

"Okay," she said as she was opening the front door.

"Have a blessed day!," he said to her just as she was walking out.

"You too, my King!"

After she left, K'von went into the kitchen and opened the fridge to grab his favorite juice: Dole orange, pineapple, strawberry and banana. He poured himself a glass and downed it; he was in hurry.

He grabbed his Benz car keys and walked out the big, oval-shaped glass front door. It was sunny out; he stood there in front of the door and took a deep breath, raising his face to the beautiful, early-morning sky. "Thank God that I'm blessed, " he said to himself.

He knew in his heart that everybody who got into the drug game didn't make it in the game as long as he had—nor were they all fortune enough to make large sums of money, or own properties and businesses like him. So, he felt the need to thank God. After giving thanks to God, he got into his Benz and drove off.

When he got to the end of his long driveway, he stopped to make sure no other cars were coming before he pulled out into traffic. While he was driving he opened up his CD case to find something to listen to. He grabbed his Rick Ross CD, "God Forgives, I Don't".

He popped it out of the case and put it in the CD player. He went right to one of his favorite songs on the album, "Three Kings". When the song came on, it put him in a whole 'nother mode. A 'Boss' mode. As he drove down the freeway smiling, he was interrupted by a phone call from Meechie. "What it do, family?" K'von said. " Don't tell me you back already?"

"Yes!"

Meechie wasted no time filling him in on the details about his trip to Waterloo.

"So, you believe this place is an asset to our empire?"

"Yes, big bro. It's a city of milk and honey for sure."

"You sound like you done fell in love with that place already."

"I'm not going to lie bro, I have fell in love with the money to be made in that city—not the city itself. You know our motto, Purse first, big bro," Meechie said.

"Not to change subjects, but my reason for calling you this early was because I have a problem".

Meechie was just informing him about Smoke G and his girl getting robbed. He was mad at C.K for not calling him when it happened.

"Talk to me!", K'von said.

"One of my workers and his girl were robbed for $10,000 and 50 pounds of Kush while I was in Waterloo."

"Do he have any clue who robbed him?"

"He thinks he recognized one of the intruder's voice. Somebody's got to pay; we need to make an example out of those who tried us! So how do you think I should handle it?" he said.

"First, I want to say that I am so glad that you have your crew under control—that they didn't go out and do something stupid that would have brought heat to the organization," K'von said. So, what I'm about to say to you is just me making a suggestion. I'm not looking to talk you out of anything you already set your mind to do; but I suggest you just fall back just for now. What was taken from him is not something that will hurt our empire—and it's not something that we are going to allow anybody to do and get away with it, either. So, give it a few months...you know the streets will tell who they were. Once we find out, *then* we hold street court on whoever did it."

"What you said make a lot of sense, big bro," Meechie said.

"See, in these streets you got to think like a boss. Make conscious choices, and not emotional choices," K 'von said to Meechie.

"Alright. Talk to you later, family member," Meechie said. When K'von got off the phone, he turned his music back up and got right back into his boss mode.

His first business stop was the barber shop to see how things were going. Since Meechie out of town handling his business, business still had to go on at the barber shop. K'von got his Uncle Ray, who used to run a barber shop back in the day, to take over until Meechie finished handling business out of state. When he walked into the barber shop, his Unc was sitting in a chair reading the newspaper.

"Good morning Unc," he said, then shook his hand.

"Good morning to you too, nephew."

K'von then walked over to the customers and shook their hands too. It was a gesture of saying 'I appreciate the money that you put in my pocket' without saying it verbally. That was one of the reasons why he was so successful in the game; he made people feel like it was okay to give him their money. He treated people with respect, no matter who they were or what they had.

"How things going?"

"Everything going according to plan," Uncle Ray said.

"If it starts to get overwhelming, just let me know."

"Nephew, I got this, but if it does, you'll be the first to know."

The two of them sat there and kicked the shit.

"You know nephew, this new generation of kids are different."

"Why you say that Unc, did somebody disrespect you since you been here?,"
K'von asked in a defensive voice.

"No, not at all. You know, since I took over for Meechie I have been able to talk with the kids more, and hearing them talk, and seeing them come in and out of this barber shop—smelling like weed, with no regard of how it will affect others. Son, they done gave up on themselves and life. As they get their hair cuts, listening to them tells me that they don't even value their parents, or their elders."

"You know Unc, you're right. But one has to keep in mind that there is no real leader or role models to look up to; these kids look to find role models, and the only ones they are going to find nowadays is hustlers, pimps, drug dealers and gang-bangers," K'von said.

"You're right, nephew," he said. "And that's where you come in at."

"I'm not following you, Unc."

"What I'm saying is that you need to open up something like a Big Brother and Big Sister program."

"I'll look into that," he said.

"Well, it was good talking to you, and if you need anything let me know."

"Alright, Cat-Daddy," his Unc said.

"You went really 'old skool' on me with that one, Unc. " After sitting at the shop talking with his uncle, it was time to go check on his other establishment. He got back in his ride and headed over to the Laundromat to see Mo'tik.

When he walked through the front door, Mo'tik was helping an elderly lady carry her clothes to the car. He held the door for the lady.

"Thank you, son. You're such a gentleman," she said. "I'll tell you, they don't make them like you two anymore nowadays."

"I agree with you," they said.

"It's because we were raised by good, strong, loving women," K'von went on to say.

"Son, you have a wonderful spirit, and may God watch over you despite your wrong," the lady said.

By that time Mo'tik had closed her trunk.

"It was nice meeting the both of you," she said.

"Nice meeting you as well," they said.

As she was walking away, K'von and Mo'tik looked at each other. "Are you thinking what I'm thinking?"

"About doing something nice for her?," Mo'tik said.

"Yes," K'von said.

The two could tell the elderly lady didn't really have too much by the old, beat-up car that she was driving. Just as she was about to get into her car, K'von said. "Excuse me, mama."

"We would like to bless you with something," Mo'tik said.

They both reached into their pockets and peeled off a grand apiece, and gave it to the lady.

" Young men, I can't take this from you guys," she said.

K'von insisted that she take it. "Please, you must take it— just consider it a gift from above."

The old lady was so happy that she started to cry. "You guys just don't know how much this means to me...I been behind on some of my bills for a few months now, and this money will help me pay them—and I will have some left over to buy groceries."

The both of them were so touched by what had just taken place, they too wanted to cry.

"We are all about giving back," K'von said to the lady.

"God says He love a cheerful giver," Mo'tik added.

'That's right, son," the lady said.

The lady thanked them again for their act of generosity.

When the little lady left, Mo'tik said, "Man, I feel good doing that for her. I'm not going to lie, it almost brought tears to my eyes."

"I must admit, I was touched by it too," K'von said.
They then went into the office to go over the books and to talk about life itself, family, and other things. While they were discussing business, Mo'tik asked K'von, "what's your plans for later on?"

"I'm taking my girl to the Bulls vs. Miami basketball game tonight. Do you and your girl want to go? I would love it. The ladies can catch up on each other's lives, and we can kick it. The game starts at 7 o'clock, so meet us at the front entrance at 6:30. I'll see you then," K'von said, and headed for the door. He then drove over to the car wash to see how things were going with Moe. The two of them went into the office and discussed business.

After about 45 minutes they were finally done; Moe leaned back in his chair and asked K'von if he wanted something to drink.

"Nah, I'm alright. What are your plans this evening?," K'von asked him.

"I have no plans, why you ask?"

"Well, me and my girl, and Mo'tik and his girl are all going to the Bulls vs. Miami game tonight, so I was wondering if you and you girl want to come?"

"Of course, we'll go."

"I'm going to tell you what I told Mo'tik: meet us at the front entrance at 6:30 pm."

"We'll be there," Moe said. They shook hands, and K'von left.

About 20 minutes later he was pulling into the clothing store parking lot. Once he found a space, he parked his car and got out.

Fab saw him walking up and met him at the front door.

"What it do, fam?"

"How things going here at the store?," K'von asked.

"Man, business has been booming since we got all our spring and summer items in. You know these niggas are ready to impress these ladies this summer, and the ladies are ready to show off their asset as well," Fab said.

"Fab, you're something else, bro."

The two headed into the office to talk. "Voo, take over until I get back," Fab said.

"Okay, boss."

While they were discussing business, K'von asked Fab if he wanted to go to the Bulls and Miami game along with him, Moe, Mo'tik and their girls.

"Most definitely," he said.

"We'll all meet up at 6:30 at the front entrance."

"I'll see you all there at 6:30 then," Fab said.

K'von rose from his chair, the two shook hands, and he left.

CHAPTER 17

When K'von got into his car and started it up, he looked at the clock on the dash, which said 10:45. He pulled out of the parking lot and headed for the freeway, on his way downtown to do some shopping.

He found a place to park, then headed into the Gucci shop to grab a new Gucci bag for Precious.

After looking around the store, he found what he believed to be a perfect bag for Precious. He paid for the Gucci bag and left the store. When he got back into his ride he called Meechie to see if he wanted to go to the Bulls vs. Miami basketball game; he had already asked everybody else except him. Meechie answered his cell.

"Fam, do you want to go to the Bulls vs. Miami game tonight with the rest of the GMO family and their girls?," K'von asked.

"Nah, but thanks for asking!," Meechie answered. *"Me and my girl had already made plans to watch a movie with the kids."*

"Alright! If you need me, you know how to reach me. Talk to you later, Bro," he said.

"One love, fam," Meechie said.

While he was driving down the freeway K'von began to yawn, so he decided to go back to his mansion to take a nap. He pulled into the driveway, put the car in park and turned off the engine. When he walked inside he took his shoes off, went upstairs, and stretched out across the bed to take a nap.

It was 5:00 when K'von got up from his nap. Precious was just coming up the steps, and when she walked into the bedroom he said, "I got surprise for you, so close your eyes until I tell you to open them."

He went in the closet and grabbed the nicely-wrapped box containing the latest Gucci bag. "No peeking," he said, just as he was about to walk out of the closet. He walked over to the bed where she was and said, "You can open your eyes now."

"What's in here?"

"You'll see when you open it up."

She started opening the box, and when she saw it was the new Gucci bag she hopped off the bed and gave him a couple of wet kisses on the lips.

"Thank you, daddy!"

"You're welcome!"

"I'm going to wear it to the game tonight," she said.

"It's almost 5:30 so let's go take a shower, because you know how long it takes you to get dressed," K'von said.

They went into the bathroom and showered, then got dressed so they would be on time to meet the other couples at the front entrance of the stadium as planned. When they left the house it was 6:00.

When they arrived at the stadium Fab, Moe and Mo'tik and their girlfriends were already there waiting on them. They all went inside the stadium to watch the game.

While the heads of the GMO were at the Bulls vs. Miami game, and Meechie was at home with his family having family night; on the west side of the city—over in the hood where the thugs and soldiers hustle to make their living—C.K. and some of the GMO's craziest goons were planning a blood bath.

They were planning to kill one of the guys who robbed their boy Smoke G for 50 pounds and some cash, and neither Meechie nor K'von knew anything about their plan. Once C.K had gotten wind of one of the guys who had robbed his best friend Smoke G and his girl, he'd taken it upon himself to make sure that revenge was handed down personally. He and some of the GMO goons were planning to take down the one who had robbed Smoke G. C.K had information on a few of Kam's hangout spots, and intended to follow up on his leads. After following up on his leads and coming up empty-handed, there was one more place that CK and his goons hadn't checked, which was this local hole-in-the-wall bar. He knew if him and his goons went there looking for Kam it wouldn't be a smart idea.

After the Bulls vs. Miami game was over the four couples went to a sports bar that had a bowling alley in it where the couples order drinks, food and bowled a few games.

Later on that night, around midnight, C.K.'s sent his two sisters, Megan and Stacey to a local hole-in-the-wall bar; C.K. had heard that the place was a regular hangout for Kam, one of the guys who'd robbed Smoke G and his girl. The two of them went to the bar looking for him, hoping they could lure him back to their house so that Kam could receive the consequences for the choice he made to rob Smoke G. Remember, you're only free to make choices, but you're not free from the consequences of those choices you make.

When the ladies got to the bar, Kam was nowhere to be found. Instead of leaving right away, they decided to wait around to see if he would show up. They ordered some drinks and proceeded to wait to see if he would show up at the bar.

After spending time drinking and laughing at the cats in the bar trying to holler at them, the two realized they'd been there for over an hour, and still no Kam.

"Let go," Megan said to Stacey, "he's not coming."

"I'll tell you what, if he doesn't show up within the next half hour, we are out of here," Stacey said.

"Alright!," Megan said.

They ordered one more drink and after they finished them, Stacey said, "let's go."

After hanging around the bar for a few hours the two were calling it quits.

When they got to the parking lot, there were a guy smoking on a blunt.
Guess who it was? None other than Kam. '
'Hey ladies," he said as they were walking past him. Not wanting to draw any attention to themselves, the two kept walking.

"You two ladies are too good to speak to me?," Kam asked.

"Nah, it's not that—I'm kind of heated right now because we were supposed to meet a friend here, and she didn't even show up," Stacey said.

"I'm feeling you baby, I would be heated if someone stood me up too," he said. "Hit this blunt, maybe it will cheer you up a little." He passed it to her and she took a puff. "How you feeling now?"

"Much better," Stacey said.

"By the way, I'm Kam—and you two fine ladies are...?"

"I'm Stacey, and this here is my best friend Megan."

"Nice to meet the both of you. What are you beautiful ladies plans for the rest of the night?," Kam asked.

"We don't have anything planned since our friend stood us up," Megan said. "What, you got something in mind?"

"Yes, I do.''

"Like what?"

"The three of us can go back to my place—or yours—and smoke some of this fire-ass Kush that I'm blowing on right now, and I got a couple of bottles of champagne in the car that we can sip on, too."

"That sounds like a good plan, there's nothing else to do," Stacey said.

"Are you cool with it, girl?"

"What about you?," she asked Kam.

"I'm down with whatever, I just want to have some fun," Megan said.

"How about we go back to our crib?—that's if you don't mind, Kam," Stacey said.

" Not at all," he said.

"You ladies lead the way and I will follow," he said.

See, when a man thinks with his 'little head' and not his brain, this is what happens.

He could be walking into a trap, just to have sex with a woman. Like the old saying goes, 'all money ain't good money'—and every time an opportunity arises to have sex with a woman is not good for you. Being thirsty for sex can sometimes get you killed.

Megan and Stacey got into Stacey's truck and Kam followed them. With Stacey behind the wheel of her blue Dodge Durango with tinted windows, Megan got on her phone and called C.K. When he answered, she said "the trap has been set, and he took the bait".

"Yes," C.K said, then hung up the phone.

After he hung up, he began to put his plan in motion. He and five of his craziest goons from their 20-man crew of mostly juveniles grabbed some guns and headed over to Megan's crib.

When the two women made it to their house they didn't know for sure whether C.K and his boys were already in the house or not.

Stacey pulled into the back yard of their crib and parked the truck. Kam parked his car on the side of her truck and the three of them went inside.

"You can go downstairs in the basement and make yourself comfortable, we'll be right down after we slip into something a little bit more comfortable and appealing to your eyes—if that's okay with you," Megan said.

"No problem," Kam said with a smile.

Stacey turned on the basement light for him and he walked down the steps. They checked the bedrooms to see if C.K and his goons were there. The first bedroom they went into was Stacey's; C.K and his guys were there, dressed in all black with guns in their hands—ready to handle their business.

The ladies went into Megan's bedroom and stripped down to their panties and bras, then went into the basement to join Kam. When Kam saw them, his eyes lit up. He was taken aback by what they were wearing, which caused him to choke on some blunt smoke. Once he caught his wind he said, "Look at you ladies, looking all sexy."

The two of them walked over to the couch and sat down next to him. Kam passed the blunt to Stacey and she took a puff, then passed it to Megan. After seeing them in just their bras and panties, Kam started to get relaxed. He popped open a bottle of champagne and took a sip from the bottle. "So, what do you ladies want to get into tonight?," he asked, then leaned in for a kiss from Stacey. She was okay with kissing him, since she was doing this for her brother C.K. While they were kissing, Kam's hands were all over her body. As they kissed, Megan intervened and said, "How about you take your clothes off so we can have some real intimate sexual fun."

He stood up from the couch and the two women started to undress him with his back turned toward the basement steps, Stacey in front of him and Megan in the back.

Stacey started to unloosen the button on his pants and Megan began taking off Kam's shirt, but she was having a hard time getting it over his big-ass head.

The whole time this was going on, the only thing on Kam's mind was that he was about to have sex with the both of them; it never crossed his mind that he was being set up.

When Megan finally got his shirt off and he turned around, there was C.K and his goons staring at him, along with

Smoke G who he'd robbed. His eyes got so big, you would have thought he'd seen a ghost.

See, you can't just do anything you want to somebody and not expect to answer for what you've done.

The girls ran upstairs. C.K grabbed the bottle of champagne and cracked Kam upside his head with it, and he fell to the ground; C.K and his goons began to punch and kick him. He cried as he was dragged up from the floor.

"You piece shit motherfucka, you done robbed the wrong one this time!," C.K said.

"I'll give it all back. I promise I will fix it, just don't kill me!," Kam said.

"Well, you can start by giving me the names of the other persons that were with you on the night of the robbery."

Kam paused; he couldn't give up his own brothers. He'd rather for his mother to go to one funeral instead of three. " I can't do that," he said.

"You know if you don't cooperate with me, you're going to die, right?," C.K told him.

"I don't' know their names," he said.

C.K had had enough of his games. Torture him until he tells us the name of his partners and where the cash and weed is at!," C.K snarled.

As they were torturing him, Kam kept trying to plead with C. K. and he said, "I've heard enough from this piece of shit scum bag."

When he said that, Kam just knew that his life was over.

"Smoke G, come here," C.K said. He walked over to C.K.

"Get one under your belt," C.K. said, and handed him the shotgun.

Smoke G didn't hesitate to pull the trigger. The first blast from the shotgun was a head shot. Blood splattered all over the wall, but that wasn't enough for Smoke G; he shot him once more in the stomach. When the girls heard the shots, they came running down the stairs and they couldn't believe what their eyes saw. C.K started barking out orders.

"Go get some bleach, a bucket of soapy water, some towels and a mop," C.K said to Stacey. She ran up the steps to retrieve those items.

"Why are you guys just standing around?" C.K said.

" What do you need me to do?," Megan said.

"Go look outside to see if you see anything suspicious."

As Megan went upstairs to check if there was anything suspicious going on outside, Stacey was coming back down the stairs with the towels, bucket of soapy water, bleach and mop. They started to clean up their mess.

"Take some of them towels and wrap them around his head to stop the blood from running all over the place," C. K said. Stacey grabbed the towels and started to wrap them around Kam's head. Everybody else started to clean the blood splatter off the walls. C.K. had them wipe off everything that was in the area where Kam was executed and mop the blood off the floor. Once they were done, C.K. sat down in a chair, looking lost about what to do next.

"What are we going to do with the body, C.K?," one of the shorties asked him.

"I never thought that far," he said.

He then got up from the chair and began to pace back and forth. After pacing for a few minutes he stopped and said, "I got to make a call." He pulled out his phone and called Meechie.

"What are you doing calling me this late?," Meechie demanded.

"Fam, I can't talk over the phone, but I need you to come to my sisters' crib right away."

Meechie knew right away that it had to be something very serious.

"I'm on my way," he said, and hung up.

He got out of bed and went into the bathroom to get himself together. He threw on a jogging suit and tennis shoes and left. He hopped in his low-key car, a Chevy Malibu. When he got to the sisters' crib, he knocked on the door and C.K opened it. He had a weird look on his face.

"Let's go downstairs...I got something to show you," C.K said.

The two of them started walking down the steps; when Meechie got downstairs, everybody was standing in front of the body so he really couldn't see it right away.

"What going on, guys?"

They all stepped back, and that's when he saw the dead body; Meechie couldn't believe his eyes. He went right into boss mode.

"Let me tell you all something right now: none of you better not say a word about what took place here tonight, to anybody!," Meechie stated. "And if anyone of you do, then whoever spilled the beans will be killed—just like this piece of shit laying on this floor. Do I make myself clear?"

"Yes," they all said in a scared voice.

He then called K'von's lawyer Jacob.

"Hello," he said in a tired voice.

"Sorry to wake you, but I need you to meet me at the spot.
"

The 'spot' was a meat locker that his father owned, where the GMO crew disposed dead bodies.

"I'll be there," he said and hung up.

"C.K., you guys load the body in the trunk of Megan's car parked out back," Meechie ordered.

C.K took an area rug out of its big storage bag; they wrapped the body up in sheets first, then put the body into the bag.

While they were putting the body into the area-rug bag, Meechie asked, "Who pulled the trigger?"

"Smoke G, the one who he stuck up for the 50 pounds and cash," C.K said.

Once the body was loaded in the trunk of Megan's car, C.K drove the car with the body in it to the dumping site. Meechie drove Kam's car. When they got to the spot, Jacob was waiting for them; he didn't ask any questions, either. Meechie and C.K. took the body out of the trunk and carried it inside. Jacob turn the machine on, and the two put the body through the meat grinder to dispose of it.

Once they were done grinding up the body, C.K sprayed the machine with a solution that had a strong ammonia odor, then sprayed it off with a water hose.

Meechie pulled Jacob to the side.

"Don't mention any of this to my brother," he said.

"Your secret is safe with me."

Then Meechie reached into his pocket and gave him $3000.

"I'll see you in my office at 11:00 sharp tomorrow," Jacob said.

"I'll be there, sir," Meechie said.

The two then shook hands, got back into their vehicles, and drove off.

"Look, you guys are going to buy Megan a new car tomorrow—and I want you to take hers and Kam's cars to J& R Scrap Iron. I'll call Mike so that he can meet you guys there," Meechie said.

He called Mike and got him up out of bed. "I'm on my way," he said.

When they got back to the house, Meechie informed Megan that she was getting a new vehicle, so if she had anything of value in her car she should get it out now. He then told C.K to handle his business, and he took two of the goons with him to meet up with Mike at J&R Scrap Iron.

When they got there, Mike was already waiting on them. C.K handed him a wad of cash and the keys to both cars; then they left. When Kam didn't come home that night, his girl called his mother to see if he had spent the night over at her house. When she said no, his girl said, "I been calling his phone, and he hasn't answered any of my calls. That's not like him. Something is wrong."

"I'll call the police station to see if he got arrested," Kam's mother said. When she called the police station, they told her that no one by the name of Kam has been arrested in the last 24 hours or 48 hours. The officer was nice enough to let her file a missing person report over the phone.

Remember: when you rob somebody—even if you got away that day or night—that doesn't mean it's over. Just when you think that shit is over, somebody will be standing right behind you—waiting to pay you back in full when you least expect it!

CHAPTER 18

Precious woke up early that morning because she had hired a fitness trainer to help her get in great shape for her wedding, which was six months away. Precious got dressed and drove to the fitness center. While she was in traffic K'von woke up and he reached as he had become accustomed to for Precious ass. His hands fell on a cold sheet and he remembered that she went to the gym. He got out of bed and proceeded to get dressed because he had to meet up with Meechie and his lawyers, and stop by the club to check and see if Big T and the rest of his employees were doing their jobs. It was Friday and the club was expected to be packed; he wanted to make sure he had enough of everything he needed for the packed crowd.

Precious pulled into the parking lot of the fitness center, excited and ready to workout. She got out of her truck and walked toward the front door, calling her fitness trainer on the phone. *"I'll meet you at the door"*, he said.

The two introduced themselves and got right down to business. On her first day, the trainer had her run three miles on the treadmill.

When she was done she was exhausted. She got off the treadmill and grabbed her bottle of water. She sat on the bench and relaxed her body, which was soaking wet from the workout.

"Come on, we got more to do. We got to hit the punching bag and the weights," he said.

Precious looked at him then popped open her bottle of water and took a big sip and relaxed. While she was relaxing, she could hear her phone ringing in her workout bag. She just ignored it. When it rang a third time, she grabbed the bag, unzipped it, and grabbed her phone. When she saw that it was her sister Ashley, she answered it.

"Hey Sis, Aunt Helen is in the hospital. "

"What happened to her?"

"She fell out in the kitchen while cooking."

"What hospital is she at?"

"Memorial Hospital."

"I'm on my way."

"Hurry up, because the doctor said it's not looking too good for her."

Precious grabbed her workout bag and bottle of water and ran out of the gym. She jumped into her Jaguar truck and made a mad dash for the hospital. Her heart was pumping faster than normal. Her leggings and tee shirt were drenched in sweat, and she just couldn't get there fast enough; the rush-hour traffic was a nightmare.

People were driving bumper-to-bumper, including her. Traffic began to speed up some time later, and when she thought she had an open path she punched it, but a car came out of the other lane and she had to slam on her

180

brakes. She looked through her rear view mirror. The two cars behind her slammed on their brakes too, almost running into her and each other, but no one was hit. She leaned her head back against her headrest.

"Thank you, God!," she said. She grabbed her phone and called K'von.

"Hey babe, what up?," he said when he answered.

"I just called to say that I love you."

"I love you, too!"

"Where are you at?," she asked him

"I'm at my lawyer's office with Meechie." K'von could sense that something wasn't right. *"Is everything alright?,"* he asked.

"On my way to the hospital."

"Why are you on your way to the hospital? Are you sick?"

"I'm fine! It's my Aunt Helen...she was just admitted, and she might not make it," she said, with tears streaming down her face.

"Sorry to hear that, I'm on my way right now. What hospital is she at?"

"No, you don't have to do that; I will call you once I find out her condition."

"Keep me posted, my love."

She entered the hospital through the emergency room, and was told what room her aunt was in and how to get there. She ran to the elevator, but it was too slow coming down so she took the stairs instead. She had her keys and bottle of water in her hands as she cleared two steps at a time. When she got close to the room she could hear crying, and when she walked into the room there was her sister, crying her heart out. She looked around and saw Precious.

"Aunt Helen is dead, Big Sis."

"Don't say that," Precious said.

The doctor had been in the room and spoke up.

"It's true," he said. "We did everything we could to try and save her, but the heart attack she had was so massive that there was nothing we could do."

"Thanks Doc," Ashley said.

She looked at Precious, who was now crying her eyes out too. She put her arms around her and hugged her. "It was just her time that all. She's gone to Heaven to be with God."

"Can I see her before I go?," Precious asked the doctor.

'Yes, you may come right this way."

He escorted her to the room where the body was being held. She looked at her and said, "I love you, Mama Helen."

She and Ashley cried all the way back to their vehicles. As soon as Precious got into her truck, she called K'von. He was still at his lawyer's office and when he saw that it was Precious, he stepped out of the room to take the call.

"She didn't make it, babe," Precious said as soon as he answered.

"Sorry to hear that. Are you still at the hospital?"

"I'm on my way home," she said.

He hung up the phone and walked back into his lawyer's office.

"Sorry, I'll have to excuse myself due to a family emergency. I'll get up with you later, Meechie. Jacob and Fred, give me a call to let me know how thing went."

He left in a hurry to be with his girlfriend. He got into his car and headed to the house. On the drive to the house, he couldn't help but think about Helen; he couldn't believe that Helen was dead. Her death had him thinking about his mother and how it would affect him if he lost her.

He pulled into the driveway and when he walked past Precious' truck, he noticed that she was sitting in it crying her heart out. He opened the door and hugged her.

"Let it out, I know it hurts because I'm hurt too."

"She's gone, K'von," she cried. "Why did God take my mother, father and now my Aunt Helen?"

He didn't know how to answer that question; so, he remained silent.

After sitting in her truck for 30 minutes or so, the two decided to go into the house. He helped her up the stairs and into the bedroom. He took her shoes off and tucked her in bed.

"I'm right here by your side if you need me, my love. Is there anything that I can do for you? Just let me know."

"Just hold me, K'von," she said, and he did as she asked him.

"Has anybody called to let Marquis and A 'Lexus know about Helen?," he asked her.

"No, we haven't; we want to wait until A 'Lexus gets back from spring break tomorrow so we can sit down with the both of them. That's when I'm going to break the bad news to them both."

"That's understandable," he said.

K'von knew he had to be at the club later on that night, so he called Big T and told him that he needed him to keep an eye on the club because he wasn't going to be available tonight.

"No problem, Boss," Big T said.'

"I trust and believe that you can handle it, so, don't let me down," K'von said.

"I won't, Boss.'"

Once he hung up the phone he called his mother and Meechie to fill them in on what was going on. Right before he hung up from speaking with his mom, she said, "Son, tell Precious that I will keep her and the rest of the family lifted up in prayer."

"I will, Mom."

Precious was the love of K'von's life, and he felt sorry having to watch his girl deal with the death of her aunt-mother.

Over at Ashley's house she held her phone in her hand, debating whether she should call Marquis at school and A'Lexus , who was out of town on spring break, to let them know about Aunt Helen. She and Precious had agreed not to tell either one of them until A 'Lexus got back from spring break. But she thought that if it was her, she would want to know right away. She couldn't build up the courage to do it; after thinking it through, she thought, *what if A' Lexus had a nervous breakdown after hearing the bad news about Aunt Helen—with nobody in the family there to console her?*

While she was at home grieving over her Aunt-Mom's death Tray was blowing up her cell phone. She decided to answer; he had called about 20 times.

"Hello," She said, in a depressing voice.

"Is everything alright, sweetheart?"

"Yes!"

"It doesn't sound like it, are you sure?"

She didn't want to worry him with her problems, so she withheld the truth from him. After a few minutes into the phone call, she couldn't hold it in any longer and started crying.

When she explained to Tray what had happened, he said, "I'm on my way over to your crib."

He got into his vehicle and drove to her condo to show moral support.

He was there in no time. She heard a knock at the door and went to open it. She looked out of the peep hole. When she saw it was Tray, she opened the door and let him in. He grabbed her and put his arms around her tightly.

He walked her to the couch and the two of them sat down. She started to tell to him about her Aunt Helen, whom she saw as her mother.

"She died in the hospital from a heart attack today, Tray."

He sat there and listened to her, consoling her while she dealt with the pain of losing her aunt.

"I would like for you to spend the night with me, because I don't want to be alone tonight," she said.

"I can do that," he told her.

After crying for more than an hour, Ashley decided to go take a shower and left Tray downstairs watching TV.

When she was done showering she came back into the living room and asked him if he wanted something to drink.

"Do you have any red wine?," he asked.

"Yes." She went into the kitchen and grabbed a bottle of red wine and two glasses. The two sat there and drank almost the whole bottle. Ashley was hoping that the wine would help drown some of her pain. After almost finishing the entire bottle Ashley said to Tray," I've had enough, what about you?"

"Me too," he said.

She grabbed the bottle of wine and glasses and took them into the kitchen. She wasn't gone for more than a few minutes and when she returned Tray was butt naked, standing in her living room. She dropped the piece of candy that she had in her mouth.

"What do you think you're doing?", she asked Tray, who by that time was drunk.

"It's time for us to get intimate," he said.

She couldn't believe that he was thinking about sex at a time like this. She looked down at his manhood and smiled. He walked over to her and kissed her. She closed her eyes and allowed his lips to press into hers. He held her tightly and tongue kissed her. She could smell the wine on his breath.

"I want to feel you inside of me," she said.

He lifted her up and she wrapped her legs around his waist. She could feel him getting harder and harder as he carried her into the bedroom. When they got to the bedroom, he laid her on the bed and continued to kiss her all over.

He slowly pulled her lingerie over her head, then put his mouth on her chest. Her body began to clench as he worked his way down her body; she got hot when his tongue went inside of her intimate area, and she began to moan as he sexually pleased her. The fact that she hadn't had sex in about a year, she had forgotten how good it felt when a man goes down on you.

"Do you have a condom?," she asked him.

"Yes, I do." He grabbed his pants and reached into his pocket for a condom. Once he had the condom in his hand, he sat there on the bed just staring at her.

"What are you waiting for, put it on," she said.

He tore the condom package open and put it on. When his manhood entered her intimate area, she jumped.

"Take it slow," she said.

He slowly began to make love to her. All you could hear was her moaning and the smell of sex in the air. The two made love for the first time that night, off and on for hours. Even though the way their first sexual encounter came about wasn't under the best circumstances, it still ended up being a wonderful experience for them both.

CHAPTER 19

Ashley woke up bright and early the next morning; she pulled the drapes back in her bedroom to let the sunlight in then called her sister Precious to check on her.

They talked for about an hour or so on the phone, discussing their plans for the day. Their plan was to stop by the school to get their brother Marquis, who was in college and pick up their sister A'Lexus at the airport.

Right before Ashley hung up, Precious asked her to call Nia and ask her if she would watch over the salon for the next few days. As soon as she hung up from talking with her, she called Nia.

"Good morning, girlfriend," Ashley said.

"Good morning to you too, Ashley!"

"Nia, I'm calling because Precious wanted to know if you would manage the salon for a few days."

"I can do that for her, is everything okay?"

Ashley did not want to tell her best friend about Helen passing away at that time. "Yes!," she said. "The both of us have some important family business to attend to right now."

"Well if you guys need me just give me a call."

"Alright, girlfriend take it easy," Ashley said.

When Ashley got off the phone, she went into the kitchen to cook breakfast for herself and Tray, who was still in the bed asleep. The smell of her cooking breakfast found its way upstairs and into Tray nose, causing him to wake up. He climbed out of bed and grabbed his overnight hygiene kit, then went into the bathroom to freshen up. Once he got himself together he went into the kitchen to join his girl.

When he walked into the kitchen he kissed Ashley right on those big, sexy lips of hers. "What an amazing night it was last night," he went on to say.

"You can say that again," she said.

"So, are we officially together now or what?," he asked her.

"That's a good question; I guess so, since I done gave my 'goods' up to you last night."

Those were the words that he had been waiting to hear come out of her mouth.

"That's what I'm talking about," he said, right before he smacked her on her juicy backside.

Breakfast was done and they sat at the table to eat. While they were eating Ashley said, "I want you to know a thing or two about me. I'm not the type of woman to give it up that easy, it's just that I really like you. Plus, the fact that I was dealing with the death of my aunt, and you being by my side showing moral support...I just felt that it was the right time. So, don't take it the wrong way and think that I am easy."

When she finished talking he looked her in the eyes.

"I know you are a good woman and I would never think that, Ashley. Trust me, what happened last night was meant to happen. I really, really do like you. I'm falling head over heels in love with you already, and I question myself; but I knew why I was falling so fast for you. It was because I've been asking God for a good woman. A woman whom I could spend the rest of my life with."

Tray was laying the charm on heavy, for sure. She was eating out of the palms of his hands. His mission was accomplished; he had her smiling, and that's all that mattered to him.

"Do you really mean that, Tray?"

"Yes! I mean every single word of it. Ashley, you're the kind of woman that every good man dreams of marrying. You're a good woman, you're smart, down to earth, loving, driven, and beautiful."

When he was saying all of those things about her, she wanted to cry. For some time now, Ashley had wanted a good man who loved her for her—and not for what she had. She believed that she had found him.

Ashley was really feeling Tray, and she was falling in love with him faster than she thought she would have.

After breakfast Tray went into the bedroom to get dressed. He had to go home and change so that he could then go and manage his car lot.

"I will check on you throughout the day and if you don't mind, I would like to spend some time with you later," he told her. "We don't have to go out, we can stay in the house; I just want to hold you and be there for my beautiful queen, if it's alright with you."

"I have no problem with that," she said. "Tray...there are some things that I need to say before you leave, so I'm going to be straightforward with you. In my last relationship, my ex cheated on me, and I don't think that I can deal with being cheated on again. So, if you know that you can't be faithful to me, then don't start something that you can't finish—because if you cheat on me, I'm going to get my sister's man and his crew to make you pay."
She quickly put her hand over her mouth, because she hadn't wanted to say all of that to him. "Sorry Tray, it just slipped out. "

"There's no need to apologize, babe. I know it came from a hurtful place because of your past relationship. I get it! I know how you feel, because I too have been cheated on before. And after feeling that pain, I vowed to myself to never inflict that pain on anyone," he explained. "So, your heart, mind, body, and soul are safe with me. I don't want to hurt them, I just want to love, protect and enjoy them."

"Awww, that was so sweet, Tray," she said.

After the two finished pouring their hearts out to one another, Tray got dressed. Right before he left, he gave Ashley a passionate kiss then walked out of the door.

CHAPTER 20

Over at K'von and Precious' house, K'von had stepped outside to his car to make a phone call. It felt like perfect timing, because Precious was lying in bed dealing with the death of her aunt Helen.

He opened up his secret compartment and grabbed his other phone; he called Vee to let her know what was going on, but she didn't answer so he left her a message.

"Hey Love, if you can't reach me for a couple of days or so, it's because I just had a death in the family; but I will call you as soon as I can. Love you." Then he hung up.

When he got off the phone he put it back inside of the secret compartment, and went back inside the house.

Later on that day, about 1:00, Precious got out of bed because she had to pick her sister A 'Lexus up from the airport at 2:00.

She had to make two stops before picking her up from the airport. She had to stop by her sister Ashley's crib first, and the second stop was at the college to pick up her brother Marquis. She had less than an hour to do all of this. She and Ashley were going to sit down as a family and tell the both of them about Helen. She got dressed. When she finished, she called Ashley to let her know that she was on her way.

"I'll be ready," she said, and hung up.

When she came down the stairs and K'von saw that she was fully dressed, he said, "Where do you think you're going?"

"I'm going to pick Ashley up, we are going to swing by the college to pick up Marquis, then the three of us are going to the airport to get A 'Lexus," she said.

"Do you want me to drive?," K'von asked, being that he was concerned about her safety.

"Trust me, I'm okay to drive. Thanks for asking."

"Alright then, I'll see you when you get back home."
He walked her to her truck where the two shared a kiss. He opened the door for her and closed it after she got in. She started up her truck and he stood there in the driveway as she drove off.

He was concerned about her, but since she was gone he saw it as an opportunity for him to meet up with Meechie so he could re-up; he was ready to go back to Waterloo to chase that cash. He called him and told him to meet him at the spot.

While Precious was driving, she began to think about how she was going to break the bad news to her brother and sister. She thought about doing it over lunch or talking to them back at the house. When she was a few blocks away she called Ashley to let he know that she was close. When she pulled up to her condo, Ashley was looking out of the front door. When she saw the truck pull up, she came out of her condo.

She locked her front door, walked to the truck and got in. Precious drove off as if she was in a hurry.

"Call Marquis for me, please?," she said.

Ashley dialed his number and when he answered, she said, 'Big bro, what are you doing?"

"Nothing much, just hangout in my dorm room with some friends."

"Well, me and Precious are on our way to pick you up so we can spend some quality time as a family, which is something we haven't done in a long time."

"That sounds cool to me."

"We're not that far away, so be ready," Ashley said.

"I'll be waiting for you guys I love you, sis, and tell Precious I said I love her too."

"I will. We Love you, big bro," Ashley said right before she ended their call.

As soon as Ashley hung up the phone she said, "Marquis told me to tell you that he loves you." Precious just smiled!

Other than that, their ride to the college was mostly quiet. About fifteen minutes later, they were pulling into the college parking lot and Ashley called her brother to let him know that they were outside.

He came right down and got into the back seat of Precious' truck. He then leaned over the seat and gave both of them a kiss on the cheek.

"Good to see you guys, I sure missed spending time with my sisters."

"We missed you too," Precious said.

While they were pulling out of the parking lot he asked them, "where are we going?"

"To pick up A 'Lexus at the airport," Ashley said. "She went to Florida for spring break with some of her friends."

"How has little sis been doing?," he asked.

"She's doing good in school, and she's been looking for colleges to attend. You know she just turned 18 two days ago."

"Enough about her, what's been going on with you two?," Marquis asked.

"As you know, I'm still working at the salon doing hair and going to school get my real-estate license. I also have a wonderful boyfriend now," Ashley said.

"What about you, big sis?"

"Nothing new, really, other than I'm getting married in less than six months—and I'm pregnant," Precious said.

"Congratulations!," Marquis said.

"Thank you!"

Then out of nowhere Marquis said, "what's really going on? Something is really wrong, I can sense it. Is everything okay?"

Before they could answer, he said, "by the way, I tried to call Aunt Helen, and she hasn't been answering her phone. Has either one of you guys talked to her lately?"

"No, I haven't," Ashley said.

"What about you, Precious?"

"I haven't talked to her lately, either."

Just as he was about to say something more, Ashley said, "we're at the airport."

"I can't wait to see little sis," he said.

"She's not little no more, she done got taller and put on some weight since the last time you saw her," Precious said.

They pulled up to the front entrance and there she was, waiting for them. The three of them got out of the truck and gave her a hug. Marquis grabbed her luggage and put it in the truck. They all got into the truck and drove off. Right away, A' Lexus could sense that something wasn't right.

"What's going on?," A'Lexus asked. "Why did all three of you come to pick me up from the airport?"

Ashley couldn't hold it in any longer; she began to cry.

"Helen is dead."

Marquis' and A'Lexus' mouths just dropped open.

"What happened?," Marquis said.

"She died of a heart attack two days ago," Precious said.

"We wanted to tell you guys, but decided it was best if we told you at the same time, in person. I hope you guys are not mad at us," Ashley said.

"Aunt Helen is gone," Marquis said. "What are we going to do?"

"We are going to be strong, because we got each other to look after."

"Mama Helen was good to us all," A 'Lexus said. "I'm going to miss her."

"We all are," Marquis said.

"What restaurant do you guys want to eat at?," Precious asked them.

"I don't want to be bothered with any people other than family right now," A' Lexus said.

So, they stopped at Wings & Wings to pick up some food, then they went back to Precious house where the four of them cried and talked about memories each of them had of Helen. After spending several hours together as a family, Precious dropped A 'Lexus and Marquis off at Helen's house. On the drive to drop Ashley off at her condo, she began to tell her big sister about her new man.

"Precious, our relationship is too good to be true. The fire between us is hot, but sometimes, sis, I be thinking that one day he is going to call me up and say 'I don' think this is going to work out'. "

"Girl, you shouldn't think like that!," Precious said. "You can't let your past relationships affect your current relationship."

"That's what I've been doing, too," Ashley said.

"Have some faith, Ashley," Precious said.

"I should; he is the perfect gentlemen. He calls me at work just to hear my voice. No man has ever been that kind to me. When we go out to the movies, or to dinner at a nice Italian restaurant, an elegant lunch at a quiet French hideaway he takes care of the arrangements and everything else. And I love all those things about him, too."

"He sounds like a nice guy, Ashley."

"He is, and deep down inside I believe that he is the one."

"If you believe that, then why are you allowing your past relationship to cause you to doubt?", Precious said.

When she pulled up to her condo, they hugged each other and Ashley got out of the truck. She waved at Precious as she was driving away. Ashley opened her front door and went inside. She went straight to her bedroom to take her clothes off then got in the shower. When she was done showering, she put on her pajamas and grabbed a book to read. She wasn't reading the book for more than ten minutes before Tray called.

"What are you doing sweetheart?," he asked her.

"Just sitting in the bed reading a book. What are you doing?," she asked him.

"I'm sitting on my couch thinking about you."

"Oh, really! What were you think about?"

"How I wish I could hold you in my arms right now," he said.

"If you want to come over just say you do."

"I want to come over," he said.

"I don't know...the last time you were over to my place, you tried to fuck my brains out."

"I would like to do that to you every night, but tonight I just wanted to hold you in my arms."

"Can you do that?," she asked him.

"Yes, I can do that for you, babe."

"So, what's taking you so long to get over here then?"

"I'm on my way," he said, and hung up the phone.

CHAPTER 21

A week after Helen had passed away, everybody was preparing to go to Helen's funeral and Meechie hadn't made it back from Waterloo yet. K'von called him.

"The Funeral is in less than two hours, where are you?"

"I just pulled into my driveway, me and my family will be on time."

"Thanks for making it man, you know if you didn't, it would have crushed the family's heart," K'von said.

"Let me get ready and I'll see you at the church," Meechie said.

K'von had make sure that Helen left this earth in style and with love. He had called all the people that he knew to come out to see Helen off to heaven. Even though he wasn't into God like many of his family members and others that he knew, he was still aware of God's words, which he learned from the time he was a young kid; it wasn't until after the death of his daughter, Kristie that he started to shy away from God's word.

On the way to the church K'von stopped by Helen's friend Katherine's house to pick her up because she didn't have a ride to the funeral.

"You look sharp, young man," she said when she got into the car.

"Thank you!," he said.

"So do you, Mrs. Katherine."

On the drive to the church K'von called Meechie to see where he was at. He didn't answer; he, his girl Paris and his two sons were already at the church.

When the two of them pulled up to the church, there were cars parked two blocks away and people were still coming and standing outside, trying to get in. K'von and Katherine went around the back of the church to park in the area reserved for family. He parked his Benz and he and Katherine went inside through the back door.

When he walked inside and saw Meechie, he smiled and walked over to him. Everybody walked off to let the two talk in private.

"Man, this is a sad and depressing day," Meechie said. "So many people were affected by Helen's death. She was good to a lot of people. There was nothing that she wouldn't do for anybody. If you were hungry, she would cook you something to eat. If you needed a ride, she would give you one. If you needed money and if she didn't have it, she would call one of us to get it. Everybody in the neighborhood loved her especially the kids," Meechie said. "How's Precious taking it, K'von?"

"Meechie, she's taking it the hardest out of her family. Helen was her aunt and mother after her mother and father passed away in a car accident. It was Helen that stepped up to the plate to take care of Precious and her three other siblings when she didn't have to. And for that reason alone, Precious has been forever thankful for her doing that. She has shown her in many ways that she appreciates what she did...Man, look at all these people in here," K'von said.

After they were done talking they went to find their girlfriends. As they made their way through the crowd Meechie spotted them sitting in the front row. Since there was no room for them to sit, they sat in the back pew of the big, packed, wall-to-wall church, looking up at the altar. The flicker and glow of the candles that lit the faces of the saints lining the walls cast an eerie quality over Union church.
The church was where Precious had attended for as long as she could remember; she sought comfort in the quiet shelter of the church where she had first entered on the day she was baptized. She had spent many hours there helping out her mother and the elders of the church. Church was her safe haven.

She sat in the front of the church, staring at her aunt lying in the coffin, who had been a gift from God for her and her three other siblings. The preacher walked up to the podium and began to speak of Helen.

"This was and still is a wonderful child of God who laid her life on the line to do God's will in this life," he began. "God has seen her works by faith, but He has now called her home because her work here on earth is done. Thank God that she's on her way to Heaven to be with Him and Jesus

Christ, who sits on the right side of the Father. So, for all you that are hurt, I understand; but there is no need to be when you understand how God works. He's the one who gives life and takes life for a purpose. Sister Helen's purpose by God was fulfilled. So, if you are going to shed some tears, let them be tears of joy. Sister Helen knew what real joy was—Jesus, Others and Yourself—and she lived it," he said. "So wake up, O sleepers, rise from the dead, and Christ will shine on you. Amen!," he said as he ended Helen's eulogy.

Afterwards, the six pallbearers carried the coffin bearing her body and put it in the black hearse. Precious, Marquis, A "Lexus, Ashley and a few family members road in the hearse to the cemetery. On the ride to the cemetery, tears flowed from Precious and her siblings. Once they arrived at the cemetery, family and friends gathered around Helen's coffin as she was lowered into the ground. As it was lowered, more and more flowers were thrown onto the coffin while Precious read a poem called "Do Not Stand".

Do Not Stand
Do not stand at my grave and weep
I am not there. I do not sleep.
I am a thousand winds that blow.
I am the diamond's glint of snow.
I am sunlight on ripened grain.
I am the autumn's gentle rain.
When you awaken in the morning's hush,
I am the swift uplifting rush,
of quiet birds in circled flight.
I am the soft stars that shine at night.

So do not stand at my grave and cry
I am not there; I did not die.

After Helen was buried the family and friends gathered at a place called Sara's Catering to eat and socialize.

When you lose a loved one, it hurts. But always remember that, though they might be absent from the body, they are still present in spirit and in memory, which doesn't have to ever pass or fade away.

CHAPTER 22

It was Sunday, and Mo'tik was having his usual Sunday dinner with his crew, where he rented out the restaurant for the day for his crew members and their ladies to enjoy a meal together as a family. He was running late, and everybody was already at the restaurant waiting for him and his girlfriend Gwen.

When they finally entered the restaurant, everyone was drinking champagne or wine. They were laughing and talking, having a good old time. Mo'tik and Gwen walked over to the table where the whole crew sat. He pulled Gwen's chair out from beneath the big oval-shaped table, smiling as if everything was just fine. Then all of sudden, he said, "What the fuck did I tell you, Pokey?! "

"What are you talking about, family?"

"I told you not to make a move on the guys that disrespected you at the mall the other day when you and Streets were together," Mo'tik said. "Did I, or did I not?"

Pokey didn't say a word.

"I asked you a question, Pokey."

He just sat at the table, eating some hot wings that the chef was planning to put on the menu for the first time.

"Get up," Mo'tik said in an angry voice. This was not like Mo'tik, to act outside of his natural calm and collected character like that in front of company who wasn't employed by the GMO family.

"Now, since you reacted against my orders, we have a problem on our hands. They know you did it, so they are going to be gunning for you—and now the team has to be at war about something so simple that could have been handle in a better way!" The whole room was as quiet as a church mouse. Mo'tik walked over to where Pokey sat and slapped his plate of wings off the table onto the floor. Since he'd disobeyed a direct order, Mo'tik was going to make him pay.

"Now get down on your knees and eat."
Everybody looked at him like he was out of his mind.
"I said eat!"
Everybody thought he was just playing around, until he said it again.
Pokey got down on his knees; he grabbed a wing off the floor, put it in his mouth, and started to eat it. Everybody watched him do it.

"You're wrong for that," Pokey's girlfriend said.

"Bitch, since you want to put your nose in my business, you get down there and share a meal with your man."

"What we got going on has nothing to do with my woman," Pokey said, speaking up for his woman. "This is between me and you," he said to Mo'tik.

"You're so right," Mo'tik said, "she should have thought about that before she decided to insert herself in grown men's business. Now it's too late for her."

Both of them were on their knees eating chicken wings off the floor as they were being humiliated; everybody watched them. Those who were in the room watching it transpire knew better than to speak a word about it, no matter how they felt.

When the chef came out of the kitchen and saw them on their knees eating off the floor, he turned right back around; he didn't want any part of that.

After Pokey and his girlfriend took a few bites off the wings, Mo'tik said,

"Get up off of the floor, the both of you." He then had the nerve to say to Pokey, "Don't you ever let a man or anybody degrade you, especially in front of your woman or family." He hugged Pokey and his girlfriend. "Now let's eat. Where's the chef at?," Mo'tik said.

The chef could hear him from the kitchen, and opened the door so fast. "I'm right here," he said.

"Is the food ready?"

"Yes, it is Mo'tik."

They all sat at the round table to eat like a family. Mo'tik was acting as if what he had just done was okay. As for Pokey and his girlfriend, they were upset; Mo'tik had humiliated the both of them in front of their friends. They sat at the table with their lips poked out. Everybody else at the table was eating, drinking, talking and laughing. Enjoying themselves. Every time somebody at the table would laugh or whisper something to one another, Pokey automatically thought they were laughing and talking about him and his girlfriend eating the wings off the floor.

When the Sunday family dinner ended, they all left the restaurant.

When Pokey got in the car, his girl was still fuming from the degrading stunt that Mo'tik had pulled back in the restaurant, so she didn't say a word.

"What's the matter?"

"You know what's the frikin' matter. You let that piece of shit-ass motha'fucker degrade us in front of all them people! When he told me to get on the ground and eat the food with you, you should have shot his ass right in the face."

Since Pokey didn't stand up for himself or her, when they arrived home his girl went into the bedroom and grabbed a pillow off the bed; she then went back into the living room and threw it at him.

"Since you allowed another man to treat you as if you were inhuman, and treat us both of as if we were animals, you can sleep on the couch tonight!" She turned around and went back into the bedroom and slammed the door.

CHAPTER 23

K'von and Precious were at the house spending some time together. The two were in their movie theater room watching a movie. Halfway into the movie, Precious started to feel sick.

"Bae, I don't feel so good," she said.

"What's the matter?," K'von asked.

"I feel light-headed...like I had to vomit."

Being the caring and loving man that he is, he picked her up from the chair and carried her up the steps to the bedroom. He pulled the cover back for her and she laid down. "Is there anything that I can get you, my love?"

"Yea, could you get me a glass of orange juice please?"

He went downstairs to the kitchen, opened the fridge and grabbed the orange juice.

He grabbed a glass from the cabinet shelf and poured her a glass of juice before putting the orange juice back in the fridge. When he walked back into the bedroom, Precious was lying on the floor. He dropped the glass of juice and ran over to assist her.

"What's the matter,?" he asked, concerned.

" I don't know, but something is seriously wrong."

"I'm taking you to the emergency right now. "

He helped her get dressed, and out the door they went. On the way to the emergency room, she began to break out in a sweat.

K'von put his foot on the accelerator. When he pulled up into the emergency room entrance, he rushed to the passenger side and help her out of the car. By that time, a nurse came running toward them with a wheelchair. She held the chair while K'von helped Precious into it. The nurse wheeled her in. Once she was checked into the emergency room, she was taken to a room.

About fifteen minutes later the doctor came into the room and he asked her all kinds of questions.

"Well, I would like to run few tests and see what I can find out," the doctor said.

He had the nurses draw blood from Precious' arm. An hour later when the doctor came back into the room, he said, "something is seriously wrong."

"What is it Doc?," K'von said. He was even more concerned now.

"Are you sure you two want to hear this?," the doctor asked.

"Yes, but let me sit down first," K'von said.

The doctor smiled. "She's 6 weeks pregnant, that's all."

K'von's mouth dropped when he heard the news. He couldn't believe what the doctor had just said! He thought he was dreaming.

"Say that one more time, Doc? "

"You guys are having a baby."

Precious was so happy that she started crying.

"Aren't you going to congratulate me?," Precious said.
K'von got up from the chair and walked over to the bed; he kissed her.

He was so excited about the news that he wanted to let the tears roll down his face, but he didn't. As a youngster, he was taught to never let a person see him sweat or cry. Even though this was a time to allow someone whom he loved see the tears of joy fall from his face, K'von couldn't ignore the street code even over the love of his unborn child.

The both of them sat in the room talking about babies' names and the sex of the baby. They both agreed on one thing: they were happy about having a baby. Precious wanted a girl, and K'von wanted a boy. He had already had a girl—his daughter China; he wanted more boys. For about an hour they talked about the sex of the baby, and names for the child if it was a girl or a boy. The only reason the conversation ended was because the Doc came into the room and told Precious she was free to go.

"Make sure you drink lots of water, no lifting more than five to ten pounds as of right now," the doctor advised.

"Doc, do you know what caused her to be in pain like she was?"

"It was due to stress, so please try not to allow yourself to get stressed, and make sure you get plenty of rest."

"Thanks for everything, Doc," K'von said.

Once she was checked out hospital they drove to the house.

On the drive back, K'von couldn't stop smiling.

"What are you smiling for, Mr. Man?"

"About us having a child together. This is something that you've been wanting for a long time, and I'm so happy that it finally happened."

"This is a perfect time because I'm receiving two things I always desired. We are planning a wedding, and I am pregnant with our child," Precious said.

"My question is this: are you going to walk down the aisle pregnant?"

"I don't know...it's too early to say what I'm going to do. Why? You got a problem with me walking down the aisle looking all fat and bloated?"

"Not at all, because I love you no matter how you look."

"K'von, you are such a sweetheart."

As he pulled up to their home and drove down their long driveway, he looked at his perfectly manicured lawn.

When the car came to a stop he got out and opened the door for her, and the two of them went inside their house.

While they were sitting on the couch talking, Precious said, "Let me call Aunt Helen, she's going to be so excited when I tell her that we're having a baby."

K'von didn't say a word, knowing that they had just buried Helen the other day.

"I'm so sorry," she said.

"It's alright baby, I know you miss her."

"I do miss her, K'von," she said, then started crying.

"Remember what the doctor told you. Don't go stressing yourself out."

"I know, I know K'von."

"Let's me help you to the bedroom so that you can get some rest."

He helped her up the stairs. When they got to the bedroom he pulled the covers back on the bed, then tucked her in. The two of them talked until she fell asleep.

CHAPTER 24

Meechie went back to Waterloo, aka the city of no love. It seemed that the name "WMF" (West side Mafia Family was going to some of the members' heads.

Since Meechie had made so much money from pushing his dope in the city of no love, he decided to give back to the citizens. So, Meechie and the WMF decided to have a cookout in Sullivan Park, and everybody in the city was welcome. The WMF had fliers made up and everything. Meechie paid some of the young shorties in the neighborhood to pass them out to people and hang them up all over the city.

Word began to circulate fast, and everybody started talking about it.

A group of females were hanging out in front of a house talking amongst themselves when one of the shorties Meechie had hired to hand out fliers handed a flyer to one of the females, who was wearing 'hoochie momma' shorts. They were so tight, you could see her fat-ass camel toe.

"What's that, Sassy?," one of the ladies in the group asked.

"Something about the WMF boys are having a cookout in the park tomorrow, and everyone is welcome."

"Who is these WMF guys? And what does WMF even stand for?, " one of the girls in the group asked.

"Like I know! I'm just as clueless as you are, " Sassy responded back. "Girl, I don't know about you, but I will find out tomorrow, because I'm up in that bitch: free food, drinks, and possibly I might be able to find me a man."

All that day, everywhere you went you could hear people talking about the cookout bash that the WMF was throwing in the park. When Meechie and the members of WMF heard people talking about it, they would smile.

The next day about noon, people were coming from everywhere to see who these WMF guys were. Kids and adults packed the park. The barbecue grills were fired up with all kinds of meats on them. Steak, chicken, hamburgers, hot dogs, lobster—anything you could think of was being cooked on those grills. For sides they had potato salad, baked beans, spaghetti and chips. They had sodas and juice to drink—no liquor, because kids were in the park. Girls were dressed in skintight outfits and outfits that showed off their best assets and their provocative outfits were turning heads. A tall, skinny older dude was standing next to this short, younger baldheaded guy and they were having a conversation when a girl walked by wearing a tank top that had her 'girls' sitting up and a pair of shorts that were hugging her apple-bottom backside; you could see her butt cheeks. The younger guy just stopped talking when she walked past.

"Man, let me get that for you, youngblood," the older guy said.

"Get what?," " the younger guy responded.

"Your jaw, youngblood." The older gentleman just laughed, because he was tickled by it.

People were laughing and seeming to have a good time. The kids were running around playing on the slides and swings, and dancing to the music; even some of the adults were dancing, too. The WMF guys hadn't even shown up yet. Trust and believe, they were planning to make their grand entrance for sure. People were laughing and having a good time. Then all of sudden, Meechie turned the corner in his black Range Rover with red leather interior and 26- inch black polished rims, along with the rest of the WMF in their Chevy's on big rims, new Cadillacs, Infinity trucks and all kinds of other 'ol skool' cars on big rims. They were coming around the bend 20 cars and trucks deep. And they had everybody's attention, too. Meechie parked his Ranger Rover and everybody else parked behind him.

Ebony, the chick he had met at the strip club called the Juice bar was standing in a crowd of chicks. "I know him," she said, "me and my girl Moo'ca had some sexual fun with him about a month ago when him and his guys came into the strip club."

"You gonna have to introduce me to one of his friends, because I'm looking for a come up. I'm tired of fucking with them same old, tired-ass niggas from the crib," Quintilla said with excitement.

"I got you, girl."

DJ Cool stopped the music when he saw them exiting out of their vehicles. WMF came up to the stage, which was the bed of a semi-trailer.

With Meechie leading the pack and J Roc by his side, they went up on stage.

What Meechie didn't know was that he was making a big mistake by doing that. He had exposed his hand right then and there; now the local dealers were about to know who was supplying J Roc with his endless supply of weed, cocaine, and molly.

DJ Cool passed the Mic to Meechie; he passed it to J Roc, and he did all the talking.

"We want to thank you all for coming out to WMF barbecue bash," he said.

"Now let's have some fun." He then passed the Mic back to DJ Cool, whom he met when he first moved to Waterloo. You should have seen the chicks—they were all over those dudes as if they were celebrities. A very attractive girl named Tasha, whose weakness was a good-looking man was standing by her cousin Ebony.

"Girl, he's fine as hell," she said.

Tasha came from a good family; her mother was a school teacher and her father was a pharmacist. She'd dropped out of college, and when she started hanging out with her 'thottish' cousin Ebony, she began to pick up her bad habits; that's when she began to change. When she made the choice to trade college in for the streets, her Dad cut her off. He was more heartbroken than anything, because he and Tasha's mother had worked hard their whole lives putting money aside so that their daughter could do something that they had been unable to do, and that was to go to college. This was something that they had always dreamed to see happen one day.

"Do you know who he is?," Tasha asked.

"Yes, I do," Ebony said with an attitude. "His name is Meechie."

Then she called his name and he looked around; she waved for him to come over to where they were standing.

"What up, Ebony?"

"Nothing much! I just called you over to tell you that this bitch is really digging you; she was about to have an orgasm when she seen you get out of your truck."

Meechie, who was a real street nigga and an all-around smooth operator for real, knew how to Mack at women.

In a deep voice, he said real smooth, "what's your name?"

"Tasha", she said with nervousness.

He extended his hand and she grabbed it. "Nice to meet you," he said.

"Likewise," she said.

Ebony then jumped in, saying, "this barbecue is off the chain! So was you guys' big grand entrance too," Ebony said.

The whole time he was talking to Ebony, Tasha was lusting over him. She was falling for him already.

"Why are you so quiet?," Meechie asked Tasha.

"I don't do a lot of talking."

"If you don't mind me asking, what do you do a lot of?" Before she could answer it, Ebony said, "Don't answer that, girl—he's trying to figure you out, with his slick ass."

"What's your problem, Ebony?"

"Your womanizing ass."

"Look here, I'm just trying to get the know her because she seems like decent person."

"Whatever, Meechie. I know you," Ebony said.

Meechie knew that if he had any chance of getting Tasha in his bed, he had to get her away from Ebony.

"How about we go fix ourselves a plate, Tasha, and get to know each other without being distracted by her?"

"I'm okay with that," she said, and the both of them walked off to go get themselves something to eat.

While they were at the grill Meechie grabbed a lobster and a steak for himself, and Tasha grabbed some chicken and a burger. Then the two of them headed over to the table where all the condiments and the sides were.

He scooped some baked beans and potato salad onto her plate, and some bake beans on his.

221

They then found a table to sit down to talk.

"You seem like a smart and intelligent lady, why are you hanging out with Ebony?," he asked

"She's my cousin."

I don't stand a chance, he thought to himself, when she said that; he just knew that Ebony had cock-blocked on him for real. So, he decided to pull a chess move on her.

"I know she had something smart to say about me, didn't she?"

"Matter of fact, she spoke highly of you. She said you were a nice guy," Tasha said.

He couldn't believe that Ebony had something good to say about him.

The chemistry between the two of them was good. They were hitting it off. During the conversation Meechie asked for her phone number.

"I don't know," she said, "I just met you."

"How about I give you my number," Meechie said.

"Let me see your phone," he said, and she handed it to him. With her cell phone in his hand, he dialed his phone number. When she caught on to what he was doing, she said, "Good one, you're smooth. "

"I guess I will be calling you or seeing you later, then," and he smiled at her as he walked away.

Everything was going good until some fool disrespected one of the WMF members. When Meechie heard them arguing he went over to defuse the situation, and the guy got smart with him. It took everything in his being not to exercise his power in the third degree on his ass.

"Look here, Slick, we didn't come here for that—we came to have a good time. I believe that you did too."

"I did," he said.

"So, let have a good time, then."

He then reached into his pocket and pulled out a blunt.

"Go smoke on this blunt, but go do it far away from the kids."

The dude took the blunt and said, "thanks, bro" as he walked away.

The law kept patrolling the area, and they were taking the license plates numbers off the vehicles from Chi town. Meechie didn't think about that when he pulled his $100,000 Range Rover up to park on display. It was starting to get dark, and they had been at the park for at least six hours, and it was to clear out. Being a respectful guy, Meechie didn't want to leave the park messy, so he paid a group of neighborhood youngsters to pick up all the trash that was thrown on the ground. He gave all fifteen of them twenty dollars apiece. They were so happy and ready to work.

One little kid was watching him as he gave the other kids the money.

"You want to get in on some of this cash too?," he asked him.

The little skinny, mean-faced kid came over to him.

"I'm not working for $20 dollars, but I will help you out for $ 30," he said.

"I'm chasing that paper just like you."

He looked at the kid and said, "I like you style, son; here's $30 dollars. Now don't you go running your mouth to the other kids about how much I gave you."

"That's snitching, I ain't no snitch."

"Look at Shorty, that's right—and don't you ever become one, either."

Later on that night, Meechie and a few of the WMF members decided to slide through to an after-hours joint where they shoot dice and play black jack. After having no luck on the dice table, Meechie went to the black jack table to try his luck there. He sat down and his phone began to ring, it was Ebony.

"Call me back," he said, as soon as he answered it. He went back to the black jack. He started off winning, but it wasn't long before his luck changed; these old skool cats started cheating him. It seemed like every time he got a good hand, one of them had a better hand. He sensed something wasn't right; he pushed his chair away from the table, stood up and stretched his legs.

"You mothafuckers are cheating," he said.

"Young blood, them are serious allegations that you are making."

He looked on the floor hoping to find some type of proof that they were cheating. When he didn't find any, he said, "It's getting late anyway, I'm out of here."

Meechie and his guys walked out the door and slammed it behind them. On their way to their ride, they were approached by this older cat. "Let me holler at you, young blood," he said. "You were right, them guys *were* cheating you. They pull that shit all the time on dudes who come here from out of town."

"Thanks, OG, I appreciate the information," Meechie said. Meechie and his guys were hot. C 'Real, being the violent one said, "I should go back in there and put a bullet in all three of them cheating-ass mothafuckers".

"Nah, we'll put something on their ass at a later date, let roll up out this joint," Meechie said.

Once they made it to their ride, they got into Meechie's truck and drove off.

CHAPTER 25

Back in 'Chi Raq', K'von was at the crib when Precious' sister Ashley came over to visit with her. When he came into the living room, Precious was telling her sister the good news about her pregnancy.

"I'll be back, I got a few errands to run," he said. He gave Precious a kiss and walked out the door.

When he pulled out the driveway into the streets, he opened up his secret compartment to check his other phone. He had 2 missed calls from Vee. He called Vee to see what she wanted.

"Hey, K'von nice of you to call me back."

The two only talked briefly because Vee had an important meeting to attend in about ten minutes.

After he hung up from talking to her Fab called, and when K'von answered he could hear loud music playing in the back ground.

"Where you at?, "he said.

"Me, Mo'tik and Moe are at my crib hanging out—just drinking, smoking and talking shit like old times. Why don't you swing thru?"

"I'll do that." He figured he could go hangout with his boys and blow off some steam.

After running errands he made his way over to Fab's crib, where he told him, Moe and Mo'tik about Precious being pregnant. The three of them congratulated him.

He had been kicking it with the fellas for about three hours when he received a phone call from Precious.

"I was calling to let you know that my sister is about to leave."

"I'm on my way home anyway," he said.

"Alright, see you when you get here."

When he got off the phone he said to the fellas, "I would like to stay and kick it, but my girl is pregnant and stressing out about her Aunt Helen, so I have to go."

Thirty minutes later he was walking inside his beautiful home. He walked to the living room where Precious and her sister were sitting.

"It smells so good in here," he said as soon as he walked in the room.

"It's this new scent called Tropical blend that I got a few weeks ago from Walmart," Precious said.

"I like it," he said.

He thanked Ashley for sitting with Precious until he made it back home.

"It was no problem, this was well overdue anyway."

Ashley got up off the couch and hugged her sister, and K'von walked her to the door.

"K'von, do you still have people who can look deeply into someone's back ground?," Ashley asked.

"Yes! What's going on?"

"I met this guy name Tray, and I am falling in love with him...I want to see if he is who he says he is."

"Give me his full name, I'll have my people do a background check on him, and I'll get back with you," he said.

"Thank you so much, K'von."

"You don't have to thank me, you're family, and that's what family do. Look out for one another." He gave her a hug, and then closed the door behind her.
He walked back into the living room.

"What were you and Ashley talking about?," Precious asked.

"Babe, that's between me and her, nosy."

CHAPTER 26

Meechie was making so much money in the city of no love from flooding the city with weed, molly and cocaine. Meechie and J Roc were hanging out at J Roc's crib counting money when J Roc got a call from Aki. He was telling him that he was about to start trial in about a month. He told J Roc that he was facing mandatory life in prison for the murder, and thirty years for 3 counts of intimidation with a dangerous weapon; but the state's attorney had offered him a plea bargain.

"What's the plea bargain?," J Roc asked him.

"50 years with a mandatory of 70%, and I will be eligible for parole after doing 35 years," Aki said.

There was a pause. JRoc asked him what he decided to do.

His response was, "I told my lawyer to tell the state to shove that plea bargain where the sun don't shine, I'm going to trial," he told J Roc.

While J Roc was on the phone talking to Aki, Meechie's phone began to ring. It was Tasha. The two were an item now.

"Are you busy?," she asked him.

"Nah, why?"

"I was wondering, what time are you coming by tonight?"

"Around 10:00 O clock."

"Alright, see you when you get here."

After he got off the phone, J Roc filled Meechie in on what was going on with Aki.

"That's fucked up, fam. Hearing that just blew my mind. Let's smoke something so I can get my mind off of Aki's mind-blowing situation," Meechie said.

After smoking two blunts of pineapple kush, Meechie stood up and said, "I'm about to head out."

The two shook up, and Meechie left on his way to Tasha's crib.

On the ride over to her crib in Cedar Falls, he was thinking about how he was going to get intimate with her for the first time.

About 15 minutes later, he pulled up at her house in Cedar Falls. When he pulled up to her crib, he saw her black BMW parked in the driveway. He called her to let her know that he was outside.

"I'm on my way down," she said.

He got out of his truck and walked up to the front door. Just as he was about to knock on it, she opened the door.

"Come on in," she said. He walked inside and she shut the door behind him. She then grabbed his hand and the two walked up the steps. When they got to the top of the steps, she said, "Now close your eyes—and no peeking, either."

She walked him to her bedroom. "Now open your eyes."

He opened his eyes, shocked by what he saw. She had candles lit everywhere, and music was playing low in the background. She even had a strobe light, which gave the room a romantic vibe.

"What do you think?," she asked him.

"I love it, Bae," he said as he walked over to her king-size bed; he sat on it, looking around the room and taking it all in. He just knew from the looks of the room that some sexual healing was going to take place. He had been waiting for this day, but he hadn't expected it to be this soon.

"I'll be right back," she said.

She left, and when she reappeared she was wearing a black, sexy bra and panty set with a pink bow on both of them. She even had on some pink heels. She stood in the door way; he blinked when he saw her standing there. She had her hair down, which came down past the middle of her back. He licked his lips, indicating that he couldn't wait to taste her. He stood up as she walked over to him. She didn't waste any time pleasing him. He saw firsthand that Tasha was the shy type out in public but in the bedroom, she would cut loose. One thing she knew how to do was please her man. Tasha believed the way to a man's heart was sexual, so she worked on mastering her oral game. She was good at what she did, but what she failed to realize was that ever man is different. She thought that all men were alike. The men that she was used to messing with were more of the straight-and-narrow type, not real street bosses like Meechie. After sampling her oral game for the first time, Meechie began to get weak at the

231

knees and he felt he was about to let loose. He wasn't ready just yet so he picked her up and laid her on the bed and he started to undress her.

He began kissing her on the neck, which was her weak spot, and she started to get weak at the knees as he continued working his way down to the middle of her chest, making his way to her thighs. He then started licking the inside of each thigh. She loved when a man went down on her, so she just closed her eyes as he handled his business. After having some great sex, the two of them took a shower and then watched a movie.

When Meechie woke up the next morning, he got dressed and she walked him to the door. When he got into his truck he checked his messages.

He had three and they were all from J Roc; he grabbed his cell and dialed his number.

"What's going on?", Meechie asked.

"I don't want to talk about it over the phone."

"I'm on my way to your spot anyway."

Once he hung up, he floored the gas pedal. He was hoping that it was nothing too serious.

When he pulled up to the house, he hopped out in hurry.

"What's going on, J Roc?"

"Last night, Slick's house was raided by the Task Force, about three in the morning," J Roc told him. "He said he had just got home, and he wasn't there no more than five minutes before his front door was ripped off the hinges by the law. The police told him that they had gotten four calls from four different confidential informants saying that he was selling crack cocaine."

"What did they get out the house?," Meechie asked.

"No drugs, but they found 5 grand."

When he heard that, he exhaled. "That's nothing. As long as nobody went to jail for drugs, the WMF family members can live another day free."

"Luckily, his girl's sister was in the house and she claimed the money," J Roc said. "Slick said he thought the money was gone, because when the law asked his girl's sister why she put the money in the cereal box, he didn't think that she was going to give them a good explanation. She said, 'I'm a guest in their home, and I was looking for a place to secure my money so I decided to hide it there. He then asked her where she got the money from. She had just got a lawsuit, so she told him that's where the money came from. They had no choice but to give the money back." J Roc explained.

"That's what's up," Meechie said. "You make sure that Slick hit her with a grand in cash for what she did for us."

"I'll make sure it gets done," J Roc said.

"I'm about to go back to the crib to visit my family and to check on how things is going with my GMO squad back home," Meechie said.

"Alright! I'll hold shit down here until you get back," J Roc said.

While on his way to the highway, he called Tasha and told her that he had an emergency back home and he had to go.

"Call me when you can," she said.

"I will," he said.

While he was on the phone with her, his brother K'von was calling him. "I'll call you back, this is my brother," he said to her, then ended the call.

When he answered K'von's call he said, "what's good, big bro?"

"I just want you to know that I talked to our sister today; she told me that mom hasn't been feeling too well, and she been hiding it from us. You know after she got out the hospital she went to see her doctor about the swelling on the right side of her neck. Her doctor diagnosed the problem simply as a virus and gave her some medication, which did help with the symptoms. The swelling lasted just a week, but it left a small knot, and the fever and sore throat recurred just recently. Since she didn't say anything else about it, I assumed that she was fine. But then I got this call from our sister telling me that the fevers and sore throat recurred. She said she called her doctor, and he set up an appointment for her to see a physician tomorrow."

"Why didn't Mom tell us what was going on?"

"I asked sis that and she said, she didn't want to worry us."

"Man, I don't know what I'll do if something happens to Mama", Meechie said.

"Me, neither," K'von said. *"Look here, she's scheduled to see a specialist tomorrow at 10:00 in the morning, so I told sis that I was coming with them. Do you want to come?"*

"Of course I do, big bro. I'm on my way back to the city and when I get there, the two of us will sit down and discuss this matter," Meechie said.

"Love you, bro!"

"Love you too, big bro!" Then the two ended their call.

Later on that day when Meechie got back in the city, he and K'von met up to talk about their mother's health problem and they both decided to go to the doctor with her as well.

You only get one mother, and one must always honor his mother all the days of his or her life. As human beings, we all know there is no one like a mother. You know how the old saying goes, *Mama's baby, Daddy's maybe.*

End of Part 1

ABOUT THE AUTHOR

I, Anthony Elmo Cole, was born in Waterloo, Iowa. When I was ten years old, my father was robbed and killed by jealous individuals because he was well off. On October 26, 2002 history almost repeated itself when I too was robbed and nearly killed by jealous individuals because I was well off.

My father's death led me to selling drugs. On my first day in high school, I was expelled for helping another of my gang brothers to jump a rival gang member. At the age of 19, I was arrested and sent to prison. In 1998, some of my best friends were killed in Chicago due to the game, and in 2003 one of my acquaintances and his girlfriend, who was 9 months pregnant, were found dead in their home. In 2004 I was sent to prison to serve a lengthy sentence.

Up until 2004, my outlook on life was centered around criminality—whether *actively,* or *mentally laying the foundation* for a future criminal endeavor. I chose to live a life of crime and mischief; needless to say, that has only provided me a career of frequent stays in the State of Iowa Department of Corrections. Over two decades of my life thus far has been spent locked down inside a prison or correctional facility. Like so many across this great country in every state, I too have been doing life in prison on the installment plan. This isn't a unique bio! In fact, it is common, and—sad as it is to say—'normal' in the lives of those individuals whose perceptions are rooted in criminal behavior.

One day after talking to my daughter Areyon on the phone and hearing her cry for me to come home, I went back to my cell thinking about how she responded to me wasting my time *doing time* in prison, and not spending it with her. After hearing her cry I felt the pain that I'd inflicted on her; it had me asking myself what I could do to improve and become a better person. I wanted to help heal her wounds and repair those damages that my actions had inflicted upon my child.

In 2005 my way of life began to change, and I gave my life to God. This was the pivotal point in my life. That was the day that my perception shifted. My story is not unique; however, what is unique is my *character*! I would like to say we are all individuals first, and perceptional people second. Perception is how we develop our personalities as well as our character: acquiring learned behavior and observations from our personal surroundings, environment, and overall interests. From that day forward I looked at my life and surroundings and the world with a new set of eyes. Now, when I look in the mirror, the man I see staring back is not the veteran, criminal-minded, gang-banger, drug dealer, manipulative miscreant that I was accustomed to seeing. What I see now is a man with life direction, life control and humility. When I view my surroundings, I no longer see a concrete jungle filled beyond its designated capacity with society's failures, or animals, or any other labels that are derogatorily placed on incarcerated individuals. What I see now are men, young and old. I see fathers, sons, husbands, and children of God. I see men who, for the most part, need a shift in perception just as I once did.

I no longer view the world as my adversary, or prey for my next assault. I see a place that I owe—big time! I see a place that holds infinite possibilities, even for someone with a history as marred as my own. On a journey to know myself I was representative of my family, and I was looking to be a leader in my community once I was released from prison. I felt it was only right to clean up some of the mess that I had made in my community. So I continue to strengthen my mind, body and soul by reading the Bible along with other spiritual books, self-help books, and taking classes that the prison offered to help educate myself.

Years later I was transferred to Fort Dodge Correctional Facility, with the mindset that the only person, thing or situation that can limit my progress in life is *me*. My new views and attitude toward life have had such a profound effect on my life, I've come to realize that others could also benefit from my journey. My epiphany gave me faith to believe that I can help others find their purpose in life and have *their* perceptions shifted for their betterment and that of their families, and society as a whole. My desire and determination to live a better, more productive and prosperous life led to one of my dreams coming true.

In 2011, my mentoring program, LEADERS, was introduced to the FDCF FORT DODGE CORRECTIONAL FACILITY. The program was created to make a significant difference in the quality of life by empowering inmates who are often forgotten by society. LEADERS stands for: Learning, Exploring, Advocating, Discovering, Educating, Righteous, Solution.

My aim and goal is simple: to spark an interest in every participant that is directed towards their own education and empowerment. Once my message was received, which was that we owe it to ourselves as individuals to lead better lives, the inmates came to the program. They learned about everything from writing a resume; starting a business; balancing a check book; establishing credit; having a will; setting goals; and exploring other important life skills including money management, bonds, mutual funds, index funds, and life insurance.

My new pastime gave me and so many other inmates a new outlook and approach to life in general. Hearing the buzz on the yard, I was being stopped by inmates who asked me about the program that was successfully influencing and motivating other inmates. I was so proud of myself for creating the program; so much so, that about a year after the program was up and running I enrolled to Victory Bible College. I graduated too, and after graduation I became second in command in the church. From time to time I would give sermons when the pastor was absent, and eventually I became head elder of the church; this is what happens when one believes in God and themselves.

I want to take this time to thank God for making this book and the LEADERS program possible; both of these things are just a testament of God's word in Phillipians 4:13 which states "I can do all things through Christ Jesus who strengthens me".

A message to all the people: remember, the true power is in the heart of those who seek to be like God. It takes the heart/love, knowledge, wisdom, understanding and the power of God to be able to build and destroy the things we need, so that we can become prosperous people in a land of milk and honey, created for us by God our Father in Heaven.

Acknowledgements to All the Players of Waterloo

Elmo, H-Town, Linbird, T.R, Chill' Will and his father Alston aka Black, Durrell, Big Bone, Allen J, Wayne, Robert Wade, B.I, D.J, 50, J Bo, Von, Nate Dog, Alex, Carlos, Oscar, Neal, Bobby Sykes, Kim Sykes, Clinton T, Romeo Sr., Just'Ice, Money, Bib, Goldmouth, Chris Roby, T Goody, Iceman, Thirsty, Doc, Dre, Brian aka B,

Schon Ray, Diddy, D Mack, Base, Worm, Moe Lottie, J.K, Moe'sal, Poony, Orintheo, Shandor, Remo, Slim, Tim Fresh, Terrell, Chuck, Cal' C, Mack 10, Tek 9, L.B,

Donshay, Fat Mack, Mr. clean, Mr. Harper, Mutter, Day Fresh, E' Sal, Trice, Tyrone, Little E, Big Carl, Pimp C, Hood Chris, Hood Boone, Hood Dirk, Hood Marlo, Hood Mark, Hood U'landice, Hood Maine, Jigga, hood Pokey, Twin, Snake, Lee Lee, Piggy, Terry, Jerry, City View Twins, Little G, Big Mike, Big Mookie,

Big Pep, Pooh Bear, Murder, Eddie West, Mark Hop, Bill Cosby, Nun, Alonzo Quinn, Malcolm, Stickman, Big Charles, Mello, Big Mon's, and all of the NFL AND Black Flag brothers, Young money, L Block, Chopper City, The Click, The Hood, D Mills, Sherman Wise, Big Moe, Big Pun.

Chicago players

C.B, Dog, Marcius Norris & Adrian, Little Greg, Nookie, Pud, Whitey, Mike-Mike, Rat, Roc, Aki, Ant, Face, Buck, Meechie, E, Reese, Chicago, Joe G, Emoe, Big Mello, Fat Pat, Silk, Smoke, Jig, Stank, Chi Town, Law, Shawn G, Little G, Big Rell, Low end, Big D, Blue, Raheem, Chuck O, Little Lord, K'von, C.K, Moe, Fab, Mo'tik, Big Q, Poppa, Goldie, L.T, J Roc, Bud, Dre, Twin, Rocky, Mighty, Deyego Monra-el.

Made in the USA
Columbia, SC
05 April 2021